Knight & Day

AN EROTIC NOVEL

KITTY FRENCH

Createspace Edition
Copyright 2013 Kitty French
Edited by Charlie Hobson
Cover by Angela Oltmann

ISBN-10: 1494488558
ISBN-13: 978-1494488550

Knight and Day is book three of The Knight Trilogy

The series is available on ebook, audiobook and paperback.

Reading order:

Knight and Play
Knight and Stay
Knight and Day

Other books by this author
Wanderlust
Blaze
Undertaking Love

Chapter One

"Anywhere."

The dark-eyed taxi driver's brows pulled together and he studied his passenger's face for a few seconds, sizing him up. Male, alone, no wedding ring, no baggage.

How wrong first impressions can be.

"San Antonio?" he suggested, his English heavily accented. "Party?"

His passenger shook his head. The last things he needed right now were the brash lights and pulsating party heart of the island's famed dance capital.

"Somewhere quiet."

He noticed the driver's brows flicker down again as he regarded him for a few more long moments before he turned away and started the engine, his mind made up. He threw the car into the erratic traffic around the airport without further enquiry.

Glad of the silence, the passenger leaned his head back against the sun-warmed seat and watched the Ibizan landscape unfold as they moved onto quieter winding roads. Lush, brilliantly green pine trees against vivid blue skies. Late spring. New beginnings.

As they rounded a bend and started to descend to the coast, the curve of an impossibly perfect bay appeared below them. Dazzling turquoise water fringed by sugar-white sands - it was a picture postcard, the kind of image used to lure tourists to part with their money for an annual week of sun-soaked bliss.

They dropped down to sea level, and the driver tracked along the sandy road that backed the beach.

"Vadella," the driver said, catching his passenger's eye in the rear view mirror. "Quiet."

His passenger nodded, grateful. A handful of restaurants and a couple of bars dotted the beach, set back from the shore, and a smattering of sun-worshippers and football-playing kids occupied the sands. Out in the bay, a few boats lazed in the Mediterranean sun, the sea barely showing a ripple. *It was as good a place as any.*

"Beer?"

The waitress behind the bar had that casual European sophistication; lithe limbed and olive skinned, her knotted, wide necked T-shirt revealing a tattoo on her exposed shoulder. She looked up and greeted him with an easy smile, offering him what he must look as if he needed. She placed a large, frosted glass down in front of him when he nodded, and he sat on the wicker bar stool and drank deeply, closing his eyes with satisfaction as the cold, fortifying liquid slipped down his throat. She was still watching him when he opened them again, her head on one side, the smile still playing around her mouth.

"On holiday?"

Polite conversation that he had no polite reply for.

"Maybe." He half nodded, half shrugged. "I might stay a while. See how it goes."

"American?" she asked, more of a statement than a question.

He nodded again. "Guilty as charged, ma'am." He touched his fingers to his forehead and gave her a small salute. She laughed softly as she wiped the uneven wooden bar top down, and for the second time that day he recognised the flare of interest in a woman's eyes. He dropped his own eyes to his beer rather than meet hers.

"So, where's decent to stay around here?"

"Depends," she said. "How long were you thinking of?"

How long *was* he thinking of? He had no idea.

"A month maybe? Two?"

She nodded thoughtfully. "There's a hotel along the bay, but it's more of a week or two family holiday place than a home. Lots of kids in the pool, that kind of thing."

She immediately registered the discomfort on his face at the prospect of making his base amongst a bunch of families. "Or we have a couple of rooms here, upstairs." Her gaze slid under the bar as she reached for a battered black leather book.

He watched her flick it open and run her unpainted fingertips down the page, tapping it slowly as she checked it. A seasoned tourism worker, her English was excellent, and she was clearly used to being asked about places to stay. The twist in her mouth told him that she didn't have good news.

"No. Sorry. We have people booked in over the next couple of days, and again on and off. You might struggle to find something free for that length of time. Unless…" Her gaze slipped past him to the beach, and she drew her bottom lip in between her teeth. "The owner of this place has a boat he sometimes lets out, but it's, umm…" she shrugged apologetically and smiled again. "I don't know the right word in English." She screwed her nose up. "It's not… very trendy, let me say it that way."

She flipped to the back of the book and checked it briefly. "It's available," she said, lifting her shoulders speculatively and raising an enquiring eyebrow for his response.

A boat. It wasn't what he'd imagined, but at least it would be solitary, no families to trip over and work around.

"Where is it?"

She nodded out towards the bay. "It's moored over there, the last boat at the far end of the rocks."

He followed her gaze, and even though he couldn't see it, he made a snap decision.

"I'll take it."

She looked surprised. "You don't want to see it first?"

He shook his head. "If it has a bed and a bathroom, it'll do me."

Something about her expression told him that she thought he ought to check it out before committing himself, but she didn't challenge him. Instead she sighed, perhaps with resigned amusement, and reached a key down from a hook behind the bar before picking up her pen.

"I better take some details, in that case." She looked up with the pen poised over the page. "Name?"

He lifted his beer, stalling. He should have thought this through more carefully. The mellow sounds of Bob Dylan floated out of the bar's sound system, the lyrics of "Like a Rolling Stone" striking eerily close to home.

"It's Dylan," he said, mentally trying the name on for size as he watched her begin to form it hesitantly on the paper. "D-Y-L-A-N."

She glanced up again, her brown eyes round and expectant. "Surname?"

His eyes slipped from hers for a second, to the neon sign bearing the name of the bar behind her. *The Happy Days Beach Bar.*

"It's Day," he said. "I'm Dylan Day."

A few minutes later, as he made his way around the rocky walkway that bounded the beach, Dylan caught a first glimpse of his new home and realised belatedly why the girl back at the bar had been reticent about leasing him the boat unseen.

The other boats in the bay were obviously either the property of well-heeled owners - gleaming white edifices of understated glamour - or else the unpretentious fishing boats of working men. *Not this boat.* No, this boat could never be accused of understated anything. This boat oozed personality.

It wasn't its size. In fact, it was quite modestly proportioned, but its size was the only modest thing about it. Where white was the order of the day for its bayside counterparts, this boat was bright orange. And yellow. And green. And red. And aqua. This boat created a faded rainbow all of its own, even though its eye-catching paintwork had definitely seen better days. Probably a good thing, Dylan reflected as he slung his bag on deck and stepped aboard. If it was this bright now, God only knew what it must have looked like when it was freshly painted. On the plus side, it had decent outside deck space and up top there seemed to be a second deck for dining or sunbathing.

That was a good thing. He planned on sunbathing.

If he'd thought the outside of the boat unusual, it didn't hold a candle to the inside. He turned the key, slid the glass side doors open and groaned out loud as he surveyed the interior, glad of his sunglasses even though he was out of the bright daylight.

He couldn't live here.

The kitchenette he'd stepped into was a canary yellow plastic and chrome affair, fifties right down to the discarded roller boots in the corner. The ship's wheel at the helm had been chromed to match the kitchen's garish decor.

It was someone's style, but it sure as hell wasn't his.

Stepping down the couple of wooden steps to his left, Dylan surveyed the living area with a slow, sinking feeling.

He couldn't live here.

Padded seating ran around the perimeter of the room, upholstered in cotton of a bright turquoise scattered with yellow lemons and bright red cherries. A well-stocked chrome and glass cocktail bar took up one wall, and hanging proud and central from the ceiling was a large, in no way understated, mirrored disco ball.

A fuck-off glittering silver disco ball. Dylan groaned out loud again. He didn't want a party boat. He cast his eyes around desperately. The door to a small, eye-wateringly lime bathroom stood open to one side, and that was it. Was there even a bedroom?

There were no obvious other doors, and he stepped back into the kitchenette to see if he'd missed it up there. Nope, no doors there either. Frowning, he leaned his back against the kitchen work surface, pushing his sunglasses up onto the top of his head.

He really didn't want to sleep on those lurid sofas.

And that was when he spotted the faded, midnight blue hatch set in the wooden floor, its surface covered in faded, swirly silver writing. Dylan hunkered down onto his haunches. The motto "Stairway to heaven" had been artistically scribed on it in antiquated metallic paint, surrounded by silver stars and moons. He fitted his hand into the curved hatch recess and pulled it up, revealing a steep little wooden staircase. Bingo. Maybe there *was* a bedroom after all.

Getting down there turned out to be interesting. It was a small, rickety stairwell, and at six feet two inches, he wasn't a small man.

Once below, he blinked to adjust his eyes. And blinked again. Where upstairs had been a bright and showy pastiche of fifties glamour, down here was definitely made for after hours lovin'.

He couldn't live here.

It wasn't even high enough to stand up in: he had to duck and crawl into the bed space.

This wasn't a bedroom. It was a goddamn sex cave… but holy shit, the bed was comfortable. He sank back onto the warm, opulent silk-padded quilt and surveyed the space.

He could sit up without hitting the ceiling. *Just.* The curved bed filled the entire lower space and the wall hugging it had been padded in deep, button-studded amethyst velvet. Lying on his back, he studied the low ceiling above him. It was… celestial. Dark inky purple decorated with luminous stars and planets, remarkably detailed and accurate to Dylan's knowledgeable eye. The same artistic, hand-painted lettering from the hatch cover continued down here on a smaller scale, silver calligraphy spelling out the names of the constellations. *Orion's Belt. The Milky Way. Ursa Major.* They all glittered down at him, and little by little the gentle motion of the boat soothed away his resistance and almost imperceptibly eased his battered and bruised heart and mind.

It was quiet, and it was solitary, and no one in the world knew he was here.

Warm and peaceful for the first time in a long time, Dylan

closed his eyes.

Maybe be could live here after all.

Just for a while, at least.

When he made his way back up on deck a little later, he breathed deeply and scanned the serene bay.

He had a new name.

He had a new home.

Now he needed a new job.

Chapter Two

Lucien walked slowly through the closed, empty club, his practised eye taking in every detail of the workmanship to ensure it met with the exacting standards he demanded for his multinational chain of adult clubs. His workmen had all clocked off for the afternoon, leaving him free to conduct a thorough inspection at leisure.

He paused momentarily beside the jacuzzi, his fingers against the cool tiles as he remembered conducting a similar inspection several years before with Sophie at his side. His cock stirred in response, and he pushed the memory aside with difficulty. Sophie wasn't due to arrive on Ibiza for a couple of days, and he missed her like hell, even more so since they'd welcomed Tilly into their lives too.

Sophie was his lucky talisman. The girl who surprised him. She still surprised him even now, after several years as a couple. Every now and then he saw a brand new side of her. She had the biggest heart of anyone he'd ever met, big enough to hold his even before he'd known that he'd given it to her.

Fuck, he missed her.

The sound of someone banging on the fire doors broke his concentration, followed by the sound of a male voice shouting outside.

"Artie, are you in there?"

Lucien frowned, crossing to the doors and leaning against the bar to open the left-hand one slowly. He dropped his sunglasses down against the glow of the low evening sun and regarded the man standing outside with his hand raised ready to knock again.

"Artie doesn't own this place anymore," he said.

The guy dropped his arm, and his whole body seemed to slump along with it.

"Let me guess," Lucien said. This wasn't the first guy to turn up in search of the previous owner. "He owed you money."

The previous owner seemed to have left Ibiza with nothing but the dodgy Hawaiian shirt on his back and a trail of bad debts in his wake after he'd hastily sold the premises and hightailed it off the island a few months previously.

The guy shook his head and leaned back against the wall of the club, his face tipped up to the skies with a resigned expression.

"No. Artie was a friend. I don't suppose you know where he's moved to?"

Lucien shook his head, noting the smooth Californian tone to the guy's voice.

"Sorry my friend. Your buddy didn't leave a forwarding address."

The stranger looked as if he'd been around the block enough times to understand the underlying meaning beneath Lucien's deliberately sparse choice of words.

He watched as the guy looked up again into the big blue expanse overhead and banged the back of his head lightly against the wall with a heavy sigh.

Something about the American's resigned, melancholy demeanor spoke to Lucien. He looked beat. Lucien had been that man, and he found himself swinging the door wider.

"You look like you could use a drink."

The guy half laughed, though his eyes were anything but amused as he nodded slowly and peeled his back off the wall.

"Too right, man. This is turning into one hell of a long day."

Lucien headed back into the club, aware of the guy pulling the door shut and following him in. He turned as the stranger's step slowed beside the jacuzzi.

"Not your usual club," he commented, as he scanned curiously over the opulent spa area they were passing through.

Lucien lifted a shoulder. "Ibiza has enough of those already."

He led the way down into the main area of the club. Behind the bar he reached for two tumblers and a bottle of vodka from a box on the floor, watching the American as he leaned against the bar and surveyed the almost completed club.

"So this place is yours?"

Lucien nodded as he headed around to stand alongside the guy, placing the glasses on the gleaming bar.

"All mine." He was as proud of this place as he was of all of the other clubs in the Gateway group. They sat in silence for a second as he poured generous measures of vodka into both glasses.

"Lucien Knight." He held a glass out.

The American nodded as he accepted the drink, and paused for a beat before he replied.

"Dylan Day." His eyes wandered over the aubergine velvet booths around the dance floor, the secluded spots, the sumptuous chandeliers. "This is some place. It holds what... about seven hundred at capacity?"

Lucien glanced up, surprised at Dylan's accuracy. "For a usual club, around that. This place is less because of the adult entertainment configuration. It tops out at maybe three fifty."

Dylan's eyes opened a fraction wider. "And it's still profitable?"

"Gateway Ibiza is club number ten, so yeah. I'm pretty confident about my business model."

"Number ten, huh?" Dylan laughed lightly. "That's impressive in this business."

"You know it?"

"Not the adult entertainment side of it, no, but I've been around clubs my whole life."

"That's how you know Artie?"

Dylan nodded. "I haven't seen him for a few years, but we used to be pretty close. He taught me how to run clubs."

Lucien regarded the other man as he looked around the club with assessing eyes, wondering if Artie's shady business conduct was one of the things he'd taught Dylan Day. He looked slightly less jaded with a drink in his hand, and from what he'd said so far the guy knew his way around a club. Gut instinct had Lucien asking more questions.

"I'm guessing you didn't come to Ibiza on holiday?"

Dylan took a long, slow slug of his vodka and set the empty glass on the bar.

"You guess right."

For the second time, Lucien sensed deep melancholy, learning more from Dylan's body language than his meagre words.

"When do you open for business? It's looking pretty shipshape."

Lucien noted the American's subject change without comment. "Four weeks."

Dylan looked directly at Lucien. "You hiring?"

"Hired, pretty much." Lucien didn't add that the only position that he was having trouble filling was that of general manager. He'd rather be on site himself for a few weeks than employ the wrong person. He splashed a second measure of vodka into Dylan's glass.

"Figures." Dylan raised his glass in a small salute, a philosophical twist to his lips.

"Is that why you were looking for Artie?"

"He knows I'm good. I don't have a resume, or references, Lucien, but this business is in my blood. I know it inside out."

Lucien didn't doubt it for a second. The way Dylan had sized the place up within moments of being inside the building had impressed him, as had the experienced eye he'd been casting over the bar the entire time they'd been sitting there.

No references, no resume. They were the kind of phrases that rang alarm bells for most people. But Lucien wasn't most people.

"I'm still looking for a manager for this place."

Interest flared in Dylan's eyes. "You won't find anyone better than me."

Formal interviews had never been Lucien's style. He operated on gut instinct, and it had yet to lead him astray.

"So show me. Three months' trial while I'm still on the island. You do it well, the job's yours. If you fuck up, I fuck up, and if I fuck up, you'll fucking know about it."

"I won't fuck up."

"Then we understand each other."

Lucien held out his hand, and Dylan shook it with a small smile that widened slowly into a laugh. It had been the shortest, coolest job interview in the world.

"I won't fuck up, man. You have my word."

Dusk had fallen over the bay by the time Dylan arrived back at the boat, and the beach was mostly deserted aside from a couple of dog walkers and a few sun worshippers who'd stayed on to watch the sunset. It seemed as good an idea as any. Dylan stepped into the kitchen to flick on the switch he'd noticed earlier with "deck lights" written on a sticker beside it.

Then, "fuck," he muttered, scrubbing his hand over the three day stubble he'd left to its own devices since he'd quit the States. Even from inside the kitchen he could see that the rails around the boat had just lit up like a Christmas tree, and not one of those tasteful minimalist ones with designer white lights, either.

Stepping cautiously onto the deck, he squinted as he took in the extent of the illuminations. Multi-coloured fairy lights twined all around the chromed rails of both decks, bright winks of pink, lime, turquoise and lemon against the darkening skies.

He should have known better than to expect understated. *Nothing* about this boat was understated.

Dylan didn't glance back towards the beach, for fear that the sun watchers had changed focus to watch his one man light show instead. He headed up onto the roof deck and opened out one of the low-slung, brightly striped deckchairs stacked up there.

He was just in time to catch the sun before it slipped down below the horizon, a golden peach blaze that cast ethereal shades of pink across the sea.

Watching nature's light show, he could feel his heartbeat slowing to the tranquil pace of the island around him.

He had a new name.

He had a new home.

He had a new job.

Maybe, just maybe, with the right wind behind him, this was going to work out.

Chapter Three

"Lucien?" Sophie's voice was eager and hopeful as she dropped her handbag on the stone table just inside the front door of the villa.

She called out his name even though she half expected that he wouldn't be there. He wasn't expecting her until tomorrow, but she'd rearranged earlier flights to surprise him.

"Lucien?" She called again, disappointment blooming in her chest at the answering silence.

"Wow." Kara followed Sophie a few seconds later, the heels of her beloved cowboy boots clicking against the polished marble floor of the entrance hall. "You didn't tell me we were renting from the royals!" she laughed, wide eyed as she lifted her shades to survey the villa. "This place is frickin' amazing!"

Sophie nodded. Kara was right, it was fit for a king. "Lucien found it." She couldn't keep the tint of pride out of her voice. Life with Lucien seemed to gild everything slightly brighter, due mostly to the fact that he put a whole lot of energy into making her happy. They'd stayed here for the first time a few months ago, back when Lucien had initially purchased this latest club. She'd been just as stunned as Kara by it, so Lucien had leased the villa for the summer, and the idea of living in it for the next few months was nothing short of blissful.

It undulated across the cliff top in complete seclusion, glistening white with more curves than Marilyn Monroe. Built on several levels into the rocks, the property meandered down towards the Mediterranean like the most glamorous tree house in the world. Private nooks and crannies scattered the grounds; secret hideaways waiting to be discovered. The underground master suite came complete with an outdoor bathroom for starlit bathing, and the sunbathing deck elevated in the trees was accessible only via a rope bridge. It was a magical place designed with hedonism and unadulterated luxury in mind, and, knowing Lucien, this was destined to be a work-hard, play-hard summer.

"Of course he did. Good old Mr. K," Kara grinned, kicking off her boots as she wandered into the huge sunken lounge, her fingers trailing over the backs of the deep suede sofas piled high with pillows. She paused by the floor-to-ceiling glass doors offering a panoramic view out over the turquoise sea. "I think I've died and gone to heaven, Soph."

Sophie thanked their driver for bringing in the cases and closed the front door, smiling at Kara, whilst thinking privately that beautiful as it was, it wouldn't be quite perfect until Lucien came home.

He'd flown out to Ibiza ten days previously, and every day without him was one too many. She missed his presence beside her in the day, and she missed his body on hers in bed at night.

Theirs had been an unconventional and emotionally fraught road to love, and the last five years together had served only to deepen the bond between them. The arrival of baby Tilly had cemented their relationship, and the little girl had very soon become Sophie's main rival for Lucien's affections. Not that she minded; it did odd and beautiful things to her heart to see her big, handsome Viking twisted around the little finger of his infant daughter.

For the next couple of weeks though, she'd have Lucien to herself whilst the baby was thoroughly spoiled by her grandparents back in the UK. Then she would join them in Ibiza along with Esther, their live-in nanny.

"Important question coming up Soph, so stop mooning over that man and pay attention," Kara said, with insight born of long experience, peeling off her t-shirt and frayed denim shorts to reveal a red and white striped bikini. Her eyes scanned the fully stocked bar. "Mimosa or mojito?"

Kara loaded the drinks tray in the kitchen ready to head out to where Sophie had set up camp beside the pool. Her friend's life had altered beyond recognition from the first moment she'd encountered Lucien Knight, and Kara's had changed right along with it. She hadn't needed to think twice when Sophie had asked her if she'd like to go into business with her, and their lingerie and adult toy boutiques were going from strength to strength. They'd established one in each of Lucien's clubs, and they were here in Ibiza to oversee the launch of boutique number ten.

Becoming a mother had necessitated Sophie taking a step back over the last year, and Kara had gladly stepped up, especially after the soap opera style drama she'd unwillingly played out with Richard last summer. Dick the Prick, Lucien had christened him, after he'd stood her up at the altar. "Should I have him killed?" he'd asked as he hugged her, and for a few long seconds Kara had actually considered it. He'd shrugged when she'd finally declined, murmuring coolly that the offer was always there if she changed her mind. Kara harboured no doubt that he was a man of his word.

She'd hit rock bottom for a while back there, and now the idea of some time away from the overwhelming support of her outraged family and sympathetic friends was one of the reasons that Sophie's suggestion of spending the summer in Ibiza had been such a welcome escape.

Sun, sand and no sex. Perfect.

Sophie was at the front door before the engine of Lucien's Ferrari had even stilled in the driveway, and she had the joy of watching the expression on his face slide from bland to unadulterated pleasure in a heartbeat. He was out of the car and in front of her in seconds.

"You're early," he murmured, his arms already around her. He lifted her clean off her feet and slipped his palms down her body until he cupped her backside in his big warm hands.

"I missed you," Sophie murmured, and saw the smile kiss his lips a second before his mouth covered hers. Five years on since she'd first kissed this man, he still had the power to melt her with just one touch, one slide of his tongue against hers. As hello kisses went, it ranked up there with the very best of them.

"I can fuck you here against the front door, or I can fuck you in our bed. I don't mind, as long as I fuck you in the next three minutes," he said hoarsely, as he pressed his body against hers.

Sophie could feel his cock straining between her legs and bit gently down on his lip with a soft laugh. "Cool it tiger. Kara's out by the pool."

Lucien groaned and slid his fingers inside her bikini bottoms. "Feels like you're ready too, Princess," he whispered into her mouth, his sure fingers stroking slowly over her clitoris until she moaned softly too. His hand lingered as he deepened the kiss, taking the time to dip his finger inside her before rearranging her bikini with a regretful sigh.

By the time Kara wandered in a couple of minutes later, they'd made it as far as the kitchen.

"Hey Mr. K," Kara grinned and stood on tiptoes to plant a kiss on Lucien's cheek. "Did ya miss me?"

"I survived," he said dryly, tugging lightly on her ponytail before slinging his arm around Sophie's waist and kissing her shoulder. "I missed Sophie more."

Kara laughed. "Get a room, love birds."

"We have one. Sophie said we can't go there yet because I have to be polite."

Sophie smacked him in the ribs and crossed to load the dishwasher, safe in the knowledge that Kara and Lucien's sparring was underscored with mutual affection.

She tuned out as they talked shop for a few minutes, Kara quizzing Lucien on the readiness of the club and boutique. Business acumen was one of the traits that bonded Kara and

Lucien as friends, and Sophie usually enjoyed the way Kara was unafraid to challenge him. But right now, her mind was on other things. As she tuned back in again she realised that Lucien had drawn his mobile out of his jeans and was talking to someone. Within minutes a driver had materialised to take an eager Kara down to the club to have a nose around, and she silently thanked her friend for her tactical withdrawal. If Lucien didn't get her alone soon he was in danger of spontaneously combusting. And quite possibly, so was she.

Kara let herself into the club with Lucien's keys, looking forward to seeing the development for herself. She and Sophie had followed it closely from back home in the UK via email updates and photos, but experience had taught them that despite the common perception to the contrary, the camera *can* actually lie. Bad workmanship could be disguised with a few carefully positioned props, and slow developments can appear faster with the right omissions and clever lighting.

She knew the club layout pretty well from studying the plans, well enough to know that the boutique lay just off to the left of the main vestibule. Kara took a moment to appreciate the effort that had gone into transforming the club's interior to meet Lucien's exacting, opulent standards. Lavish and sexy, full of the promise of pleasure with its curvy, embracing seats and sensual colour scheme, the interior already exuded the exotic glamour that so successfully seduced customers the instant they crossed the threshold.

Kara had never set foot inside an adult club before Sophie and Lucien had offered her the opportunity to join the business. She well remembered her first eye-opening visit with Sophie at her side, and marvelled even now at how what had once seemed outrageous now struck her as entirely routine. Kara had been instantly fascinated, and over the years she'd entrenched herself firmly in the world of adult pleasure, from a strictly commercial perspective. Or mainly so. It was impossible not to feel the frisson of it at times. She'd gone quickly from a toy novice to an industry expert, thanks to the trade shows and exhibitions she attended on behalf of Knight Inc., usually with Sophie at her side. They'd become well-known faces around the industry, one blonde, one brunette, one shared aim of making their boutiques a runaway success.

Kara hadn't anticipated this turn in her career, and she definitely hadn't anticipated that she'd love it so much.

Stepping through the archway into the boutique space, she was pleased to see that the progress reports they'd received seemed to have been accurate. The place was looking pretty shipshape; shelving already on the walls, velvet mannequins ready to be dressed in wisps of lace and silk, and boxes of stock lining the walls, all ready to be opened. Leaning down, she peeled the tape back on the nearest box and delved within it.

"Pretty as your ass is, sweetheart, you have thirty seconds to get out of here before I remove you myself."

Kara jumped up and twirled around in shock at the sound of the drawling Californian voice behind her. Lucien had specifically told her that the club was empty of workmen, and her heart banged hard with both panic and indignant annoyance. She had the right to be here, and this guy didn't.

"Who the hell are you?" She planted one hand on her hip and jutted her chin at the stranger. He glanced down at her other hand.

"It looks as if you got what you came for." He crossed his arms and leaned on the wall of the archway.

Kara swallowed hard and closed her eyes for a second to gather her thoughts. *Problem.* She was gesticulating at him with a vibrator. This seriously weakened her stance. She had two choices, and Kara was a woman who always came out fighting.

"This?" She held the classic vibrator up in front of her. "Oh, I don't think so. This is a beginner's tool. If I'd come here to steal sex toys I'd go for something bigger. More functions. Something like the Thor, or maybe the brand new Thor Deluxe.

It's, umm, waterproof."

He raised one eyebrow. "Your encyclopedic knowledge of vibrators tells me a lot about the state of your sex life, lady."

Kara fought the urge to shove the vibrator somewhere that would shut this guy up for a very long time.

"Managing a string of adult boutiques does that to a girl." Her voice dripped with cool sarcasm, and by the look on his face she'd made her point because he dropped the attitude and his face cleared.

"Gee, I'm sorry. You must be Sophie."

Kara shook her head. "Sophie would have been much politer. I'm Kara Brookes, Sophie's business partner. And you are?"

He paused for a beat. "Dylan Day."

"Catchy."

He shrugged.

"Well, we've established I have a right to be here. How about I give you thirty seconds to explain yourself?"

He had the audacity to laugh. "Or else?"

She could hardly remove him bodily. He was at least six foot, and by the looks of him, all muscle. Not that she'd checked him out, nor had she noticed the way his T-shirt outlined the definition of his body. Nope, definitely not. She especially hadn't noticed the tanned band of skin beneath it that had made a brief appearance when he'd pushed his hand through his too long, sandy hair a few minutes ago.

"Or else I'll…"

"Shoot me with your vibrator gun?" he suggested helpfully.

Kara sincerely wished she'd had the forethought to put the vibrator down rather than brandishing it at him some more. She was losing all the ground she'd gained.

"Or maybe you'd like to upgrade your weapon to that Thor Deluxe, given its power and all?"

Oh, he was cute. "Believe me, surf-boy, if this thing had bullets, I wouldn't think twice about shooting you right now."

He held up his hands with a disarming smile. "Don't shoot.

Lucien Knight hired me yesterday. I'm the new club manager."

Kara was aware that Lucien had been having problems filling the management vacancy. So it could very well be true. She gave him a sharp look. Dylan Day's eyes were clear of any deception. They were also piercingly green, not that Kara would confess to having noticed.

"Fine." Kara nodded, gathering herself together. "Fine. But just so you know? You're not the manager of *this* place." She gestured around the boutique with the vibrator. "I am."

He cracked a killer smile. "Suits me, darlin'. You stick to selling panties and sex toys, and leave the rest of the show to me." And with a knowing lift of his eyebrows, he turned and sauntered away.

The urge to throw the vibrator at the back of his head was tempered only by the fear that she might miss and give him the upper hand.

"I'm English!" she hurled after him instead. "They're fucking *knickers*!"

Dylan laughed under his breath as he walked back to his office. *English*. She was that all right, he'd almost sliced himself open on her cut glass vowels.

The girl was a firecracker in frayed denim hot pants, cowboy boots and a pink T-shirt that clung alarmingly to her every curve. *Move over Daisy Duke*. Her ponytail had swished like an angry cat's tail as she'd waved that goddamn vibrator around like a grade A weapon, and every word that had left that full, wide mouth had dripped sass. She was going to be a handful to work with, that much was for sure.

Closing his office door thoughtfully, Dylan realised that even though the sparks flying between them had been enough to set the club alight, the one spark he hadn't picked up on from Kara was sexual interest. He breathed a sigh of relief mingled with regret. Working relationships were best kept that way. For sure.

He'd found it pretty easy over the last few days not to react to the interest from the air hostess or the pretty waitress back at the bar.

But Kara Brookes was a whole different ball game.

Back at the villa, Lucien scooped Sophie up and carried her downstairs to the master suite.

She wrapped her arms around his neck and let him. Every now and again he needed to release his inner caveman, and she was more than happy to be in his arms.

"You decided on the bedroom rather than the front door then," she murmured, brushing her mouth over the smooth skin just below his ear.

"Call me conventional," Lucien muttered, tugging on the ties of her bikini behind her neck.

Sophie laughed softly. "That I'll never do, and you know it." Lucien was the most unconventional man she'd ever known; his unpredictability was just one of the many things she loved about him.

He lowered her onto their bed, already shedding his clothes. Sophie lay back and enjoyed the view as he peeled his T-shirt over his head and threw it aside, then moved his hands down to unbutton his jeans. He paused for a second, his eyes on her, then smiled, a slow, barely there intimacy that said *my girl*. And then he dropped his jeans, and his proud, enlarged cock told her a whole lot more about his feelings for her.

Sophie reached behind her body and finished the job he'd started with her bikini top, peeling it from her body as Lucien settled alongside her.

When he reached for her, a million sensations crowded in at once. Lust. Need. Relief. Love. Big, overwhelming, heart-scorching love. She sighed with pleasure as he loosened the hip ties of her bikini bottoms, his big body enfolding hers. He tugged the material slowly, letting it glide between her legs as his tongue explored her mouth. When he rolled on top of her in one fluid movement, his cock nestled between her thighs; hard, familiar, and all the more sexy for it. The bunched muscles of his back were warm beneath her fingers as his hands slid into her hair, pinning her in position beneath him.

"Sophie." Her name was the only word he said as he pushed his cock all the way into her with a deep groan of satisfaction that reverberated through his chest. He stilled for a moment and looked down into her eyes, and fierce, sudden emotion made her wrap her legs around him and pull his face down to hers. They didn't speak again. There was no need.

He kissed away the tears that gathered in her eyes as his hips started to thrust, slow and hypnotic. The deliberate, steady rhythm of his cock over her clitoris was in direct contrast with the fast, shallow beat of Sophie's heart. She arched, murmuring "I love you" against his neck as her orgasm snaked towards her core like quick-silver through her veins. Lucien groaned and switched from measured to forceful, demanding her all, giving her all of him in return. He was home, and therefore so was she.

Chapter Four

"Tell me again why we're having a dinner party?" Kara asked, bending down to adjust the strap of one of her high gold sandals. She'd only half listened to Sophie earlier when she'd mentioned their plans for the evening, mostly due to the fact that she'd had her nose buried in a thriller. Blood and gore. No sex. Reading about it led to thinking about it, and thinking about it led to trouble.

"It's business, mainly. Lucien wants us to meet someone."

"A new supplier?"

Sophie shrugged, reaching over and unhooking Kara's hair from where it had tangled with her big gold hoop earring. "Not sure. He was mysterious." Sophie glanced at her watch. "Right. I've got to go and check in with Miriam, make sure the food's all good to go."

Kara watched her friend's disappearing back. For mysterious, read ominous. Ominous in a…

Kara's train of thought was rudely interrupted by a thunderous crescendo of noise. She crossed to the window and craned her neck to get a better look at the visitor who'd just created his own minor hailstorm of gravel beneath the wheels of his great chunk of a motorbike. Frowning, she smoothed her palms down the short, fitted skirt of her 'when in doubt, go killer' LBD, and crossed the hallway to open the front door just as the guy on the other side pulled his helmet off his head and shook out his hair.

His sandy, surf boy hair.

Terrific. Just terrific. Kara's eyes swept him over in an instant, taking in everything from his vintage look leather jacket to the dark shirt and jeans beneath.

"Evening, English."

Lucien and Sophie appeared through the archway, robbing Kara of the chance of a sarcastic comeback. Dylan Day had the audacity to grin and tip her a private wink.

"Do come in." She smiled widely, letting her eyes shoot private daggers at him as he murmured his thanks and walked past her into the villa.

Lucien stepped forwards and shook hands warmly with their visitor.

"Sophie. Kara. This is Dylan Day."

From the look of comprehension that crossed Sophie's face, Kara knew that Lucien had already told her that he'd appointed someone as manager of the club. Sophie moved forward and placed her hand on Dylan's arm.

"I'm Sophie. It's great to meet you," she smiled, guiding him through into the lounge. "Let me get you something to drink."

Lucien's eyes lingered on Sophie's backside as she retreated to the kitchen.

"That's my Sophie." He smiled amicably, but the warning was clear in the almost imperceptible emphasis he placed on the possessive. *Look at my girl the wrong way and I'll kill you with my bare hands.* Dylan nodded. Message understood.

Kara cleared her throat dramatically, hands on her hips, her eyes wide. Lucien did a bad job of hiding his smirk.

"And this is Kara, Sophie's business partner."

Dylan extended his hand formally towards Kara with a clear, innocent as a baby smile. "It's a pleasure to meet you, Kara."

"Watch her," Lucien murmured. His blue grey eyes glittered, danger and mirth. "She has claws."

Kara opened her eyes wide and laughed lightly. "Ignore him. I'm a regular pussy cat, Dylan."

Lucien laughed low, excusing himself as Sophie called out to

25

him from the kitchen.

"A pussy cat, huh?" Dylan said. "Domestic, or wild, English?"

Kara didn't even know what it was about Dylan Day that riled her.

"Play nice, Mister, or you'll find out the hard way."

He lowered his head towards her as Sophie reappeared with Lucien close behind her, and the clean, masculine scent of him caught her off guard as he shrugged out of his jacket.

"I never could resist a challenge."

"Kara, grab Dylan's coat would you?" Sophie handed Dylan a glass of champagne and smiled at her friend, leaving Kara no option but to take his jacket or else look conspicuously rude. He handed it over with a grin.

"Don't rip it with those claws of yours."

Kara shot him a sugar sweet smile and headed into the hallway, Dylan's jacket in her hands. Faded tan and butter soft with wear, and the kind of bashed up that only ever worked with leather and spoke of many years of being moulded around its owner. It was still warm with Dylan's body heat, and as Kara lifted it onto a coat-hook the indefinable scent of him caught her for a second time.

So the man smelled good. What of it?

Irritated with herself, she rejoined the others, who by now had made their way outside and gathered on the deeply padded seats of the dining alcove beneath the shade of the awning at the back of the villa. They were laughing easily as she approached, and Dylan already looked utterly relaxed and at home alongside Lucien and Sophie. She slowed her step, watching them, suddenly unsure of her role amongst them. It looked like a table set for two couples, but there was only one couple seated at that table. Plus a couple of other people who meant nothing to and knew nothing of each other.

Dylan glanced across as she approached and pushed himself onto his feet with a wide smile.

"Kara," he murmured with a nod, catching her off guard with

both his old school manners and his use of her given name rather than 'English.'

There was something in the softness of his pronunciation that made her swallow hard, and she flashed him a quick smile to cover the inexplicable fluster he'd thrown her into. The only seat available to her was alongside Dylan on the upholstered bench-seat, and he dropped down gracefully beside her once she'd settled.

The evening sun had slipped low over the bay, and their vantage point offered them a spectacular view of what promised to be a legendary Ibizan sunset. It had been a long, hot day, and the burnt orange sun was making the most of its curtain call.

"You get some view from up here," Dylan observed, his eyes on the bay. "It must be one of the highest points?"

"Lucien likes to be king of the castle," Sophie laughed, and Lucien lifted his eyebrows as he topped up everyone's glass and then raised his own.

"To Gateway Ibiza's new management team, complete at last."

They made the toast as the caterer's waitress emerged from the villa with their first course, a platter of Iberian ham and mozzarella cheese with plump tomatoes drizzled in fragrant local rosemary oil.

"So you're American, Dylan." Sophie stated the obvious, earning herself a nod from Dylan as she pushed the platter a little towards him as an encouragement to help himself.

"Sure am."

Kara watched him place ham and tomatoes on his plate. "You're a long way from home," she said, casual but deliberate.

He nodded again, slower this time, his eyes still on his food. "I guess so. I've rented a place over in Vadella."

He looked up and smiled, the kind of open, genial smile that people employ when they really don't want to elaborate. It served only to make Kara dig a little deeper.

"What brings you to Ibiza?"

Dylan shrugged, that big easy smile still in place. "I was ready for a change of scene. I came to see a friend, but he's moved on."

"It's a long way to come on the off chance. They don't have phones in America?"

"Kara..." Lucien chided, but Dylan was unfazed by Kara's bluntness.

"Hey, it's fine. Sure, they do, but the time was right for me to move on," Dylan said, his voice not betraying any sign of Kara's line of questioning having hit a nerve. "I'd been living in Vegas a while. The place can drive you a little crazy if you let it. I'd split from my girl... it was just time."

His girl. Something about the phrase lit the fire of irritation in Kara's belly again, she couldn't have said why.

"Don't tell me. Her name was Lola, and she was a show girl."

Sophie stood up pointedly. "Kara, could you help me inside for a sec, please?"

As Kara stood to follow Sophie, Lucien pushed the platter towards Dylan for seconds.

"I never had an annoying younger sister, Dylan, but if I had to imagine what it might be like..." He looked meaningfully at Kara's back as she walked away, and she turned and shot him daggers. He shrugged, with an utterly unapologetic smile.

"What the hell's got into you?" Sophie hissed as soon as they were safely inside the villa.

Kara shrugged, aware that her behaviour had been questionable at best. "I just get the wrong vibe from him."

"The wrong vibe? Kara, we might be in Ibiza, but since when did you get vibes? You don't know the first thing about Dylan."

"Exactly! Do you?" Kara said. "Does Lucien?"

"No I don't, but I trust Lucien's judgement."

Kara trusted Lucien's judgement too, and knew that she was just digging a bigger hole by pushing her point. The vibe she got from Dylan Day wasn't an untrustworthy one. She didn't fear that he was going to rip her friends off or that he'd be terrible at his job. It was far less tangible than that. The man just somehow pushed her buttons.

Her alive button.

Her awareness button.

Her turned on button.

In Kara's book, they were all buttons that she didn't want pressed. This summer, and probably the next one too for that matter, were all about restoring her equilibrium through work and friends. Her heart had been well and truly trampled on, and it wasn't anywhere near ready to be prodded and poked by an American with a chip on his shoulder and a smart comeback always on his lips.

But Kara was ready to play nice for Sophie's sake.

"Okay." She sighed, and then smiled. "Okay. I'll be on my best behaviour. Just don't ask me to apologise for the Lola comment."

"I'd have thought you of all people would have some empathy, Kara," Sophie chided gently, handing her a fresh bottle of champagne to take outside. "He might be broken-hearted for all you know."

Kara huffed as she left the kitchen. "He doesn't look broken-hearted to me." Quite the reverse, in fact, she added, to herself.

Sophie watched her friend walk back across to the dining nook, deep in thought. Kara's reaction to Dylan Day was unreasonable, and that could only mean one thing. Hope and fear mingled together in Sophie's gut for her friend. Kara was the toughest person in the world, until she wasn't, and then she fell to pieces. But she did it in a scary, private way that allowed her to stay looking perfect on the outside while on the inside she was broken glass. Sophie knew her well enough to be sure that there were still some big, jagged shards within from the way Richard had treated her, and she just hoped her friend was not about to get sliced open by them.

Lucien glanced at his watch. The evening had settled into a more relaxed mode after Sophie and Kara had returned to the table, and for the remainder of dinner Dylan had showed himself to be an interesting and well-informed guest. His instincts told him that Dylan was a safe pair of hands for the club, and they also told him that Dylan Day was a man with a past that hounded him. He understood those hounds. He'd lived with his own pack of wolves for enough years, but he'd also learned that there were ways to silence their howls.

He dropped his arm over Sophie's shoulders and massaged her bare shoulder, the girl who held the hounds' reins and kept them at bay.

She reciprocated with a light massaging hand on his thigh as she laughed at something Dylan said, and when he slid his hand under her hair to stroke his thumb over the extra sensitive spot on the nape of her neck, she passed a hand over her forehead.

"You know guys, I might have to call it a night. I think I've got the beginnings of a headache," she murmured, her cheeks pink from champagne and Lucien's attentions as she stood up. "Lucien?"

He smiled, his fingers toying with the zip of her dress.

"I'll come with you." He placed a hand on her forehead. "We can play doctors and nurses."

Sophie rolled her eyes as he stood up and put his arm around her waist.

"Dylan, it's been a pleasure." She raised her hand to stop him as Dylan went to stand. "You guys stay a while and finish the champagne, it won't keep. I'll see you again soon, I'm sure."

As she leaned down and kissed Kara goodnight, she distinctly heard her mutter 'bitch' in her ear.

"Listen, Kara…" Dylan topped up their champagne glasses in the silence that followed Lucien and Sophie's disappearance. "I think we may have got off on the wrong foot, and for my part in that, I'm sorry."

He handed Kara her glass and picked up his own, turning his body towards hers on the bench as he settled back down. The top couple of buttons on his dark shirt were open, and Kara found her eyes following the tanned column of his neck down and wondering what he'd be like if he lost the shirt altogether.

Balls. She closed her eyes and brought her glass to her lips. She didn't want to think that.

Don't think it, don't think it, don't think it.

Maybe if she said it three times in her head something magical would happen and he wouldn't be so attractive when she reopened her eyes.

Well, that didn't work. In fact, if anything, he looked sexier still, because he was watching her, waiting for her.

"Are you waiting for me to apologise too?" she asked, placing her drink down.

"Do you feel like you need to?"

He was half school teacher, half sex god, and for some reason Kara found herself ready to be thrown over his knee and chastised for her sassy mouth. *Oh Lord. This was going to go bad.* Champagne swilled in her veins, and there was no stopping the words from leaving her lips.

"No. I actually feel like sliding over there and unbuttoning your shirt."

Dylan's expression went from lazy amusement to round-eyed surprise in five seconds flat. Surprise laced with arousal.

"Which is why you should leave *right* now," Kara continued, aware that she'd said too much, as always. Her big mouth had got her into all sorts of trouble over the years, and it would seem that this was destined to be another of those times.

She watched him swallow hard and wanted to trace her index finger down his Adam's apple.

He watched her watching him.

"Well, that's an unexpected development, English."

"You're telling me," she said. "Leave. Please?"

Kara manoeuvred herself off the bench and stood to allow him room to get out.

"Should I finish my drink?"

"Nope."

"I could take my shirt off?"

He was standing too close, his fingers on the buttons at his chest, his eyebrows raised suggestively, his expression caught halfway between joking and deadly serious.

"Goodnight, Dylan."

Kara crossed her arms firmly, and for the briefest of seconds Dylan's eyes moved down to the cleavage she'd just inadvertently served up like two oranges on a platter. She didn't dare open her mouth for fear of what might come out. "Rip my dress off and take a proper look," sprang unhelpfully to mind.

Dylan leaned down and touched his lips against her cheek; warm, tingly, and lingering for a second longer than could be deemed platonic. *Jesus, he smelt like nothing on earth. She wanted to lick his face.*

"Goodnight, English," he said softly. "I'll see myself out. And for the record… I've never felt less like leaving anywhere in my life."

Chapter Five

Dylan jerked awake just before sunrise, his heart thudding. A bead of sweat slipped down his cheek as he pushed himself up to sitting. He was alone. No-one knew he was here. He dropped back heavily against the soft pillows, forcing himself to concentrate on the constellations glowing above him, chasing his demons away across the Milky Way.

This place was different.

These people were different.

He could be different too.

Chapter Six

Dylan had forgotten his jacket.

Kara noticed it the moment she walked into the hallway the next morning. His scent surrounded her as she took it down from the hook, and it took some supreme effort not to bury her nose in it and inhale deeply.

"I'm going out for an hour. I'll see you at the club," she called through to Sophie in the kitchen, then stepped outside into the warm Ibizan morning.

Hiring the Mustang had been a no brainer. She'd listened to all of the wise advice to go for an air-conditioned saloon, and then gone merrily against it the moment she set eyes on the cherry red vintage soft top with curves in all the right places. Just looking at it winking at her in the sunshine lifted her spirits sky high, and she dropped Dylan's jacket on the back seat to take to the club.

Music on, roof down, ready to go.

Kara really hadn't intended to follow the signs for Cala Vadella, so finding herself rounding a bend and looking down over the prettiest possible blue bay came as a surprise. Or half a surprise. Or not really a surprise at all, given that she'd been the one behind the wheel. Hell, it was a small island, all the roads led to the same place. *Probably.* Feeling suddenly conspicuous in the Mustang, she slunk a little lower in her leather seat, her hands wide on the wheel as she craned her neck up the beach to see if there was any sign of Dylan.

Nothing.

She parked at the end of the bay, next to a dusty collection of cars, and climbed out, slinging Dylan's jacket over her arm as she walked slowly down the curve of local shops and restaurants that backed the beach.

Where would he stay? Villas dotted the cliffs around the bay; high end places with terraces overlooking the breathtaking view of the coast. *Was he in one of those?* She strolled from one end of the beach to the other, seeing nothing and no-one to offer any clue to his whereabouts.

The sun beat hard down on the top of her head as, unexpectedly deflated, she turned into the shade of the closest bar and ordered a tall, frothy coffee as she flicked through yesterday's newspaper that had been left on the table.

Ibiza really was the most stunning place. The sweep of sand in front of the bar looked like an office worker's fantasy screensaver, a snapshot of perfection that served as a reminder of bygone holidays.

And then that snapshot suddenly became even more perfect, because a tall, half-naked American with surf boy hair and abs to match jogged straight across it. Left to right he tracked across her vision, as though she was watching a movie. So *that's* what he'd have looked like if he'd taken his shirt off last night. Kara lifted the paper hastily, not wanting to be discovered sitting around waiting for him. *She wasn't sitting around waiting for him.* She just happened to be passing, and happened to have his jacket, and happened to spot him.

Peeping around the edge of the paper, she breathed out a slow sigh of relief. He'd passed by the bar, and was now walking along the rocks around the edge of the beach, a brown paper bag in his hand. Where was he going? There must be a pathway up to one of those villas she'd seen. She wasn't surprised. Leaving her coffee half finished, she put the newspaper back on the counter and moved outside to watch Dylan's retreating back, her head tipping quizzically to one side as he kept on going along the rocks. A frown puckered her brow. Short of diving into the water, he was fast running out of places to go. And then he stopped, and stepped sideways onto a boat moored out in the bay.

Kara squinted. And then *really* squinted. Her feet started to move before she was even aware of it, carrying her closer to inspect Dylan's unlikely digs, automatically slinging his jacket over her arm. She picked her way along the uneven path hewn into the rocks around the edge of the bay, past several impressive looking boats along the way, until she drew closer to the boat moored at the end.

Oh. My. God. What was that thing?

At that moment movement caught her eye, and she noticed Dylan up on the roof deck with his back to her. If she walked away real quiet, there was every chance he'd never know she'd been here. She wanted to do that. *She definitely wanted to do that.*

"Hey, Danny Zuko! You forgot your jacket!"

That was it. When she got home she was booking herself in to have her jaw wired together. In fact, make that a lobotomy, she'd clearly lost her marbles. Why the hell else would she be standing there like one of the Pink Ladies holding her T-Bird boyfriend's jacket?

Dylan turned, startled to hear a woman's voice, recognising it a second before he saw her. *English.*

"Some folks would consider this stalking," he said, enjoying the look of indignation that crossed her face.

"And some *people* would say thank you for returning their jacket," Kara shot back, emphasising the English word. "Nice place," she added, deadpan, casting a speculative glance over the boat. Then, *"The Love Tug?"* She read the name of the boat out loud, nodding slowly. "Well. You're full of surprises."

An illogical urge to defend the old boat rose out of nowhere, and he found himself patting the railings like the owner of a loyal pet. "She's pretty special, huh?"

When Kara nodded, her long dark ponytail bobbed like a high

school cheerleader's, and her denim mini couldn't be have been any more minimal without being a belt. She was certainly faithful to those cowboy boots. The expanse of smooth, honey-gold leg between the boots and the skirt brought him full circle, right back to those cheerleaders.

He jumped down onto the lower deck. "I was just about to make coffee to have with these." He held up the bag of still-warm Danish pastries that he'd just bought from the tiny bakery at the other end of the beach. "Join me?"

She scanned the gap between the sea wall and the boat doubtfully, and he held out his empty hand.

"I can put a shirt on, if you like," he murmured silkily as she stepped past aboard. "I'd hate you to be overcome by the urge to rip my shorts off."

Kara stomped on his foot as she passed him, her cowboy boot heavy on his sneaker as she twisted it.

"Sorry." The insincere smile that accompanied her apology said it all.

He grinned as he took his jacket from over her arm and stepped inside the cabin, nodding his head for her to follow him. She wandered in slowly, her wide eyes drinking in every bizarre detail of the place he currently called home.

Running a finger across the buttercup yellow work surface, she came to a halt opposite him.

"Is this place yours?"

Dylan could see that Kara was trying to work out if his taste ran to roller boots and disco balls.

"For now." He lifted the lid on the sugar pot and looked at her. *Fuck, she was crazy-hot.* "Sugar?"

Her presence seemed to fill every bit of the cabin with a low, simmering heat; one wrong word could set her off like a firework. She radiated energy, and being around her gave him an undeniable high.

She held up two fingers, and it took him a second to realise that she was referring to the sugar.

That was refreshing. Most girls back home would break out in a cold sweat just being near the sugar bowl, yet here she was telling him to pile it in. He picked up the mugs and glanced towards the door. "In or out?"

"Undeniably fabulous as this place is…" She cast her eyes dubiously around the cabin. "…let's go sit in the sun."

Dylan followed Kara out and gestured for her to climb the small stepladder onto the roof terrace.

"Don't look up my skirt, Sailor," she warned over her shoulder.

Dylan tried to look away as she went ahead of him and failed entirely.

"You looked up my skirt," she said matter of factly, as he stepped onto the deck and handed her the coffee mug. He shook his head and attempted an innocent expression as he opened up a couple of deck chairs and a rickety table.

"Thanks for bringing my jacket over." He sat down, ripping the bag of pastries open and spreading the brown paper out beneath them on the table as a makeshift plate. "Choose your weapon."

Kara perched on the chair opposite his, her attention caught by the still warm, sweet-scented pastries.

The girl clearly had a serious sweet tooth. Dylan tucked that snippet of information away in case he ever needed to get into her good books in the future.

"Look. I'll come straight to the point," she said, picking up a cinnamon whirl and teasing it apart with her fingers. "My shirt comment last night was… regrettable." She paused to enjoy a mouthful of the Danish, and Dylan took a slug of coffee and watched her eat.

"Regrettable?"

She nodded, reaching for her coffee. "We're going to be working together for this entire summer. We need to get along."

She lifted her eyebrows at him, looking for his agreement as she pulled off another large chunk of cinnamon whirl.

"I can see that," he said easily.

"Thing is… I'm what you'd call a 'what you see is what you get' kinda of girl, Dylan," she said. He wasn't sure whether or not she was making fun of his accent. "So I'm going to be honest from the get go, so there's no misunderstanding later."

Whoa. This girl was turning out to be freakin' amazing. A 'what you see is what you get' girl? He'd had plenty of women over the years, and not one of them could have ever been considered that.

Devious, yes.

'What you see is what I want you to see?' Totally.

"What I'm saying is this. I think you're sexy, Dylan Day." He jerked his eyes up to hers, even more surprised. "In an obvious kind of way," she added, deflatingly, then popped the last of her pastry into her mouth.

"I think there was a compliment in there somewhere," he said dryly, reaching for an ensaimada from the table.

"Yeah, yeah. But I find lots of men sexy, so it's no biggie."

"Okay then. Not so much of a compliment."

"Hey, I'm not here to stroke your ego, Sailor. I'm here to say let's not go down the obvious road."

"And that would be?"

"Dancing around each other. Pretending the attraction isn't there, and then falling into bed."

"Are you suggesting we just have sex now and get it over with?"

She placed her mug down slowly on the table and looked at him with school ma'am eyes.

"Err, no, obviously not. I'm just saying let's acknowledge the attraction like mature adults, and then agree not to act on it for the good of the club."

"I knew that was too good to be true."

She shrugged. "Are you going to eat that?" she pointed at the last remaining pastry on the table.

He pushed it towards her. "You like things that are bad for you, English."

"It's my downfall. I like sugar. I like fast cars. I like sexy men."
She licked sugar residue from her fingers, and Dylan's body
reacted with interest.

"I let myself have the sugar. And the cars."

"Two out of three ain't bad."

"Hey, it worked for Meatloaf."

"Do you always let hairy rockers from the eighties dictate who
you screw?"

"Everyone needs a yardstick. Meatloaf just happens to be
mine."

She stood up, smoothing her hands down her minuscule skirt
before holding one of them out to him across the table.

"Deal?"

*Was it a deal? Could he spend the summer around this woman without
either killing her or drilling her?*

"Should I spit on my palm before we shake?"

"That's disgusting. Just shake, Sailor."

Her hand was warm and firm, just as he imagined the rest of
her body would be if he ever had the chance to find out.

She let go of his hand. "See you at work."

Dylan touched his fingers to his forehead in salute.

He watched her pick her way off the boat onto dry land, all
long limbs and swinging hair. A pang of regret bloomed in his
chest. She was right of course, and she'd only said what he
probably wouldn't have had the good sense to.

He'd secured the management job at the club by the skin of
his teeth. Any other boss would have asked for references and
resumes. Lucien Knight had given him a shot without any of
those things, and common sense told him that any romantic
entanglement with Kara could jeopardise that trust he'd been
awarded without having earned it.

From his vantage point on the roof deck he kept his eyes on
Kara's marching figure as he drained the last of his coffee.

She passed by the small black hatchback he'd guessed must be
hers, then walked right on by the moped that would have

surprised him a little but not too much. He laughed out loud when she swung herself over the driver's door of the bright red Mustang convertible at the end of the row of shops and restaurants. Even from the far side of the beach he could hear the engine as she gunned it and left the bay in a cloud of sand.

Hell, he'd always loved Mustangs.

Kara Brookes was something else. She'd turned up unannounced, eaten his breakfast, called him sexy, and then left him for dust with nothing but a tingling palm and a growing case of frustration.

Chapter Seven

Sophie was already at the club when Kara arrived a little while later. She'd made a start on opening the stock boxes, and was kneeling on the floor surrounded by scanty lingerie and sex toys.

"Just a normal day at the office I see." Kara dropped her bag down on the floor with a grin.

"Free samples," Sophie said, holding up an edible, erect penis with a look of barely disguised horror.

"Classy," Kara laughed. "Lunch?"

Sophie made a 'no-way' face and put the choc-cock back in its box.

"Where did you get to?"

"Just giving the old Mustang a good airing," Kara said, aware she sounded vague but reluctant to mention her visit to Dylan.

"Just don't get yourself arrested," Sophie said.

Kara faked offence. "As if." They both knew she was perfectly capable of it, and she'd only wriggled off the hook one time back home because she happened to have been pulled over by a cop who'd had the hots for her in college.

"It's just that I noticed that Dylan's jacket had gone out of the hallway." Sophie didn't look up from the box she was slicing open, but Kara heard the speculative hint behind her words all the same. There was no getting anything past that girl.

"Mm. I dropped it back for him while I was out."

Sophie glanced up, her eyebrows high above questioning eyes.

"What?" Kara rolled her eyes. "You asked me to be nice to him. I was being nice."

"No, it's nothing," Sophie pulled open the carton in front of her. "It's just…"

Kara dropped down on her knees beside Sophie and reached for an unopened box, already knowing exactly where Sophie was heading with this conversation.

"Soph, don't worry. The last thing I'm interested in is getting involved, especially with some guy who we don't know from Adam. He could be a mass murderer for all we know."

"He doesn't strike me as a mass murderer," Sophie said neutrally. "I like him, actually. Easy on the eye, too."

"You think?" Kara studied the inventory list for the box she'd just opened without really taking in the details. "He's okay, I suppose."

"You suppose." Sophie smiled. "You suppose?"

"What do you want me to say? He's hot? Okay, I suppose he's hot. Kind of. If you like that sort of thing."

"You like that sort of thing."

"Are you telling me or asking me?"

Sophie placed the handcuffs she'd been examining for quality back in the box and twisted to face Kara, her hands on her knees.

"Kara. We've been friends for more than half of our lives. I know you well enough to know that Dylan Day is exactly your type, so don't even bother denying it, okay?"

Kara sighed. "Soph, I know what you're thinking, but trust me on this. I'm not about to have a holiday romance and end up broken-hearted again. See these fingers?" She held out her hands. "Burned. After what happened with Richard last year, I'm well and truly off that whole romance shtick."

"I seem to remember us having a conversation very similar to this when I separated from Dan," Sophie said, referring to her childhood sweetheart and ex-husband. It seemed bizarre to imagine that she'd ever truly loved him now, because her feelings for Lucien were so much bigger. All-encompassing.

"Yeah, but you had the delectable Lucien to pick up the pieces. There aren't enough Viking sex gods out there to go around for the rest of us."

"Or American surf dudes?"

"Whichever. My point is that after being left standing at the fucking altar in a wedding dress I didn't even fucking like all that much, I'm not about to jump into fucking bed with Dylan-yankee-doodle-diddle-Day!"

Sophie put her hand over her mouth, but the laugh came out just the same. Kara swiped her on the shoulder then burst out laughing too.

"You ladies sound hard at it."

They both looked up as Lucien appeared in the doorway with yet another box in his arms, his eyes taking in the two laughing women surrounded by handcuffs and chocolate erections. *Handcuffs. Erections.* Sometimes, it just wasn't possible to keep work and pleasure totally separate. Lucien placed the delivery down next to Sophie, and pocketed a set of handcuffs at the same time. She caught his eye fleetingly and then dropped her gaze with a discreet smile.

"Sophie, could I see you in my office in *five minutes*, please?"

She caught the emphasis absolutely clearly, and entered Lucien's office seven minutes later, deliberately missing his deadline.

"You're late."

"I was busy."

"Not just one minute late. Two." He lounged against the edge of his desk and touched the back of the swivel chair beside him, turning it slowly to face her. "Sit down."

Sophie closed the door behind her with a click and crossed the room. Lucien watched her closely, his eyes all over her. She'd dressed for him that morning, knowing full well that her feminine, not-quite demure, lace-trimmed sundress played to his cave-man instincts, and that the almost indecent underwear she'd chosen to team it with turned him hard on sight.

His hands moved warm and heavy to rest on her shoulders. Kind of loving, kind of clamped. Only the slow stroke of his thumbs on her neck beneath her ponytail betrayed him.

"Put your hands behind the chair, Sophie."

A shiver ran from Sophie's scalp to the base of her back. She swallowed, and slowly obeyed his demand. Lucien clipped the cuffs around her wrists, taking care to shackle her in place by threading the chain behind the post of the chair.

"A lot can happen in two minutes, Princess," Lucien said, letting her hair free from its band before swinging the chair around to face him. He knelt before her, checked his watch, and spread her knees.

Sophie held her breath, never sure with Lucien what would happen next.

She gasped when he rucked her dress up her thighs, his hands firm as he yanked her hips forwards on the seat. Once she was exposed from the waist down, Lucien stopped for a second.

"These are some of my favourites," he murmured, massaging a firm hand over the scrap of white lace between her legs.

"I wore them for you."

He nodded briefly, his eyes hot on hers. "I know." He gripped the edge of the delicate lace and pulled it aside, parting her thighs even wider with his shoulders as he dipped his head. He paused, his lips a whisper away from her skin. Both hands buried between her thighs, he opened her with his fingers and blew lightly over her flesh, a cool breeze to heighten the heat of his tongue.

Sophie watched him, her hands desperate to be tangled in his hair rather than behind the chair. He raised his eyes to hers and kissed her clitoris, and her body arched in response. He lifted one eyebrow, and kissed her there again. Slower, longer, with tongues, the most erotic of French kisses.

"Not just one minute late, Princess," he said, stroking one finger along her thigh. "Two."

He pushed two fingers inside her at once and fastened his beautiful mouth over her sex, his hot, wet tongue making her cry out. He mouthed her, delicate and then not so, teasing and then sensationally not so. He knew her body so well now. How to build her, how to hold her right on the edge, and how to plunge her all the way over whenever he wanted to. *He wanted to.* Her hips jerked and he followed her movements with his mouth, not letting her miss a thing.

Sliding his fingers slowly out of her, he dropped a kiss on her thigh as he straightened her clothes and checked his watch.

"One minute fifty five."

Sophie stretched when he unlocked the cuffs, and Lucien caught hold of her wrist and massaged it.

"Next time, be more punctual."

Sophie ran a hand over his crotch. "Maybe," she massaged his erection and stretched up to lick her tongue over his lower lip. "Maybe not."

She stepped away and skipped to the door, laughing when someone tapped the other side of it.

"Dylan," she smiled in welcome, straightening the skirt of her dress, opening the door wide. "I hope you're not late too. Lucien's feeling *quite* the slave driver today."

Chapter Eight

"Working late, Sailor?"

Dylan was behind the bar, bent forward over it with a look of concentration on his face and a pen in his hand. He looked up when Kara spoke and it took a second for his expression to clear into a smile. The switch from pensive to unguarded pleasure set off an unexpected sizzle of appreciation low in her gut. She pushed it resolutely aside and slid her backside onto the nearest bar stool, dropping her oversized leather bag on the floor at her feet.

"You got me," he said, rolling his shoulders back as if he'd been bent for quite a while. Kara flicked her eyes up to the ceiling to avoid staring at the strip of flesh that appeared beneath the hemline of his faded grey T-shirt. Not that the T-shirt did much of a job of disguising his body. Just the opposite, if anything; it clung to his body like lichen on a rock, reminding her all too clearly about the lean, tanned beach body barely hidden beneath the cotton.

"All work and no play will make you a dull boy," she said, wishing instantly that she had chosen a different wisecrack.

Dylan tapped his pen on the bar, looking at her for a long second. "I don't have anyone to play with tonight."

Kara shrugged. "I'd offer, but I'd probably have a drink and then start that whole 'I wanna rip your shirt off,' shizzle again, and that would be bad."

Dylan laughed softly. "I've never met anyone like you, English. Are you always this honest?"

47

"Yup. I told you. What you see is what you get."

"Okaaaay." He drew the word out, as if he were thinking how best to phrase something. "Well how about I be honest with you too?"

Was that the sound of a warning bell? Kara heard it chime loud and clear, yet she just raised inquisitive eyebrows at him.

"I like bourbon," he said. "And Mustangs. And sexy girls in cowboy boots."

The sides of Kara's mouth twitched. "Two out of three ain't bad."

"Yeah, but that's where old Meatloaf got it wrong. Two out of three *is* bad. It's frustrating, and leaves you wanting. Three out of three is much, much better."

"Or gluttony, depending on how you look at it."

"So shoot me, I'm a sinner. Come by the boat later?" His clear, green gaze was direct. "I'll cook for you."

"You cook?"

"Sure I do."

"This is the point where I should say I'm washing my hair."

Dylan walked slowly around to Kara's side of the bar and smoothed her hair behind her ear, casual yet deliberate at the same time.

"Your hair already looks pretty good to me."

Kara found herself uncharacteristically out of smart comebacks, mostly because he'd touched her and she wanted him to do it again.

He picked up her bag and placed it in her lap.

"Come around at eight."

Dylan watched her walk out, his hand on the bar stool still warm with her body heat.

Messing around with that girl was a mistake in just about every way possible. He was risking Lucien's trust, his job, and his new found peace. But he knew what was worse than all of that.

He was risking Kara Brookes.

It was that goddamn honesty thing that did it. Why couldn't she act coy, play stupid games like most other women?

Being around her was like drinking water from the clearest mountain spring. She was purity; vital, clean, life affirming. He lost his head when she came within ten feet of him. He didn't just want to drink the spring water. He wanted to bathe in it.

Kara stamped her foot down on the Mustang's accelerator, letting the wind blow her hair and praying it would blow away her stupidity along with it.

Dinner with Dylan Day? On The Love Tug? *The fucking Love Tug?*

It sounded, and looked, like the set for some cheap seventies porn flick. *Who did he think he was, Hugh fucking Hefner?* A disturbing image of Dylan wearing a red silk smoking jacket surrounded by topless Barbie girls came to mind. *The Love Tug.* The clue was in the name, and she should steer well away. She pulled along the driveway and turned the car in next to Lucien's Ferrari.

Only a few hours back she'd assured Sophie that she wasn't about to tumble into bed with Dylan Day, and here she was about to walk through the door and tell her the complete opposite.

'I'll cook for you,' turned out to be an ambitious plan. Cooking on a boat was an entirely different prospect to rustling up dinner in a conventional kitchen. Dylan was no master chef, but he'd taken care of himself long enough to be able to sizzle a decent steak. Except there was no sizzle to be had on the Love Tug – not of the culinary kind anyway - just a tiny camping-style grill and one gas ring was all he had at his disposal. *It was almost half past seven.* Unless they wanted to dine at midnight, he needed a plan B.

He cast a glance out at the restaurants dotted around the beach, their evening lights starting to glow as early diners and families sat down to eat. The scent of garlic and fresh seafood reached his nose and plan B quickly assembled itself in his mind.

Ramming the uncooked steaks back inside the unfeasibly small fridge, Dylan glanced down at what he was wearing. *Did he look okay?*

Why the hell did he feel like a teenager on a first date? He was no kid, and Kara was very far from being his first date. She *was* different though; she had him on the emotional ropes in a way that he couldn't recall being for a long time. But then life hadn't dealt him the easiest card when it came to romance, he'd been out of the dating scene for a while.

Twenty minutes later and he was back on board after a dash, empty pan in hand, to the nearest restaurant for paella, thanking his lucky stars for the laid back attitude of the chef, who'd whipped up the meal in short order with a good-humoured wink. It wasn't a moment too soon, because a flash of distinctive metallic red had already caught his eye winding down the hill towards the bay. *She hadn't changed her mind.* He'd half expected her not to come, but then in a strange way he'd known full well that she'd show up. It didn't fit well with her 'what you see is what you get' ethos not to do something she'd said that she would.

Dylan raised a hand in greeting as she made her way along the rocky path down to the boat. As she drew nearer, he had the strange sensation of regretting having asked her to come. Not because he didn't want to see her, but because he feared that he wanted to see her too much. She was stepping into his world tonight, and he knew from bleak experience that it wasn't always a good or safe place to be.

"Hey Sailor," she said, reaching out her hand for him to steady her as she stepped aboard. For a second, he fought the urge to tell her to go back. *Go back to shore. Back to safety.* And then she stepped close, and any sensible intention left his head, because she looked and smelled like heaven.

"I bought pudding." She hooked the handles of a paper bag

over his fingers.

"This is the bit where you say thank you, and then tell me I look lovely," she supplied, when he didn't speak.

He hadn't spoken because she'd taken his breath away. The girl had her own style and she sure knew how to work it. She'd somehow managed to make those cowboy boots look sexy as hell with a deep green lace dress that outlined every curve and contour of her body. With her sun-kissed skin, she looked as if someone had dipped her in gold, and hell, there was much of it on show to admire. Her dress finished mid thigh, and the curves of her breasts jiggled in greeting from her scooped neckline as she shrugged out of her tiny denim jacket. With her hair tumbling around her shoulders, the overall effect reeled him in like a fish on a line in the harbour below.

"Don't look at me like that," she said. "You unnerve me."

He snapped out of it and looked inside the paper bag. "Chocolate bars?"

"It was all I could get. Short notice." She shrugged, dropping her jacket on a stool just inside the cabin door as she moved inside. "Something smells good."

Dylan dropped on his haunches and moved the steaks in the fridge up to make way for the chocolate.

"Yeah. About dinner…"

"You didn't cook it, did you?"

"I wanted to," he said, casting a hand around the paltry kitchen. "The boat let me down, man."

"They say a bad workman blames his tools."

He held the raw steak in its packet out as evidence. "This was dinner."

Kara huffed. "Maybe it's just as well then. I'm a vegetarian."

Shit, he'd ordered mixed paella, and knew for a fact that it included chicken and chorizo.

"First rule of dating, Sailor. Check your facts."

Dylan frowned, remembering back to the dinner party at the villa. His expression relaxed.

"So. You're a vegetarian who eats ham?"

Kara's face cracked into a grin. "I had you there for a second though, didn't I?"

"Funny girl." He pushed the steaks back into the fridge and stood up. "We're eating up on deck. Go on, I'll be up there in a minute."

He handed Kara a bottle of wine, then stood back to allow her out. The Love Tug definitely encouraged close proximity, there wasn't room to swing a kitten, let alone a cat. *Did she sniff him as she squeezed by?* The overwhelming urge to drop a kiss on the curve of her neck had him clenching his teeth. He wouldn't make the first move. If his conscience was going to survive this girl, the ball had to stay entirely in Kara's court. He badly wanted her to decide to play, but she had to be the one to make a move.

She turned to him as he leaned against the open doorway.

"You know the drill. Don't look up my dress."

Chapter Nine

"Paella," Dylan said, placing the cooking pot down on the floor by his chair because the table was so small. He'd laid it earlier in the evening, or at least he'd gone as far as putting plates and cutlery out.

Kara watched him. Barefoot and beautiful in jeans and a soft, fitted white shirt with tiny, faded blue flowers on it, he was a good fit with his laid back, hippy-cool boat. To his credit he did seem at ease with the food, as he ladled delicious-looking paella onto their plates. Before he sat down to eat, he skipped down the steps again. A second later, fairy lights winked on all around the boat's railings. The effect was impossibly pretty, adding a soft haze of romance to the evening air.

Kara said, as usual, the first thing that came to mind when Dylan reappeared.

"Ah, shoot. I'm allergic to shell-fish."

She touched the shell of a mussel with her fork with a pained look.

"No you're fucking not," he said, pouring wine into their glasses. He wasn't falling for it for a second this time.

"You're right, I'm not," she said, conceding with good grace as she tested the paella. "Wow, this is gorgeous. You must give me the recipe some time."

"No can do, English. It's top secret."

Dylan only wished his cooking skills ran to such knowledge, because Kara was right, it was delicious. They ate the entire pot, and their relaxed conversation meandered lightly around topics loosely linked to work. When he opened a second bottle of wine she looked at him steadily.

"Are you plying me with wine in the hope that I'll ask you to take your shirt off again?"

Dylan cleared the plates and his throat.

"I'm fast learning not to try and guess what's going to come out of your mouth next."

Kara knew that feeling. She dearly wished she could master the art of engaging her brain before her mouth.

"Is that a bad thing?"

"No. It's a very good thing."

When he poured the wine, she sighed and raised a deliberate glance to his.

"I can't drive if I have another glass of wine."

He relaxed back and picked up his own glass. "Me neither."

Kara reached down and rummaged in her handbag, then laid her toothbrush carefully down on the table between them. She watched Dylan's face, scrutinising his expression. His lowered lashes hid it from her as he seemed to study the toothbrush for a few seconds, but when he lifted his eyes again, there was no mistaking the understanding that passed between them.

He reached into his jeans pocket and did a little rummaging of his own, then laid a silver-foiled condom packet down next to her toothbrush.

It was Kara's turn to study the table for a second before she spoke.

"Just the one?"

He settled back in his chair, then shook his head and sipped his wine.

"Whole box."

She weighed this up, then moved to kneel in front of him. Dylan was aware that a line was probably being crossed.

"I think it's probably time I took your shirt off."

A line had definitely been crossed.

Dylan widened his knees so she could move in between them.

He closed his eyes briefly when she touched the first button of his shirt. He opened them again when she slid it free, reaching out to stroke his hand down her hair as she wordlessly finished unfastening his shirt and slipped it back off his shoulders.

She'd seen his naked torso already, but it did nothing to deaden the effect of seeing it again, here and now. He had the body of a man who paid attention to detail. But not too much. Conditioned and tanned, sure, but without vanity. *Perfect.*

His shirt hit the deck, and he slid forward on the chair and moved his arms around her until he had her held against his warm, naked chest.

"You nervous, English?" He stroked her cheek with the back of his fingers. "You're trembling."

"Yeah." Kara bit her bottom lip and nodded, tentative. Then, without missing a beat, she added, "I'm nervous that you're going to be a terrible kisser."

He laughed softly, so close she could taste him, so near she could smell him, that heady scent that seemed to short-circuit her brain.

"We'd better find out then, hadn't we?" Dylan held her chin between his thumb and fingers and tipped her mouth up to his.

Slow. So, so slow, and agonisingly tender. He barely let his lips graze hers, once, then again. *Oh God.* Kara's palms were flat against his chest, enough to feel his heartbeat pick up when she opened her mouth and touched her tongue against his.

"How'm I doing here?" he murmured, smoothing her hair back from her face with both hands.

"Not bad," she whispered.

"Not bad, huh?" Kara felt his smile on her lips.

She realised a few seconds too late that she'd been hustled. He yanked her hard against him and lowered his head. This time he wasn't slow, and he wasn't tender. His mouth was hot and open over hers, and the sudden kick up from tentative to filthy had her body screaming for more. *Sweet baby Jesus, his tongue.* Kara heard herself whimper and couldn't have cared less.

The man was world class. If there were kissing medals, Dylan Day would get the gold.

He hadn't so much as touched her body yet, but she was closer to orgasm than she would care to admit. *One touch.* One touch, and she'd go.

"Undress me," she breathed, desperate to feel his skin pressed against hers.

He pushed her hair away from her ear and sank his teeth into her earlobe as he lifted the hem of her dress. Kara raised her arms above her head and let him tug it up her body. It landed on the deck on top of his shirt.

"Stand up." The raw edge in his voice made her stomach flip. "I want to see you."

She stood for him. He moved to stand in front of her. Holding her hand, drinking her in.

Standing up there on the roof deck of Dylan's boat, illuminated only by the pinpricks of the fairy lights, Kara knew without doubt that sex with this man was going to change her forever. There was no question in her mind about whether it was a good idea. At this moment, it was a necessity.

He lifted her arm high above her head and twirled her slowly around, a ballerina in a silent music box. Dancing without music, sultry and seductive.

"So lovely, English," he said softly, reeling her in against his chest. "You dazzle me."

He tipped her back over his arm and put his mouth against the hollow at the base of her throat, the heat of his denim clad crotch hard against the silk of her underwear. She gasped a little when he opened the catch of her bra. He slid his fingers beneath the straps on her shoulders, then paused to hold her close and smooch her lips a little more.

"Lost your nerve, Sailor?" she murmured, knowing full well that he hadn't, unable to resist the challenge. Dylan grazed his teeth over her bottom lip.

"Once this comes off, we're over the line," he said, his mouth moving along her jaw.

Kara played her fingers across the waistband of his jeans.

"We were over the line as soon as I stepped onto this boat tonight."

"I've been over the line since the first time I saw you," he said, and then eased her bra off her shoulders and let it fall to the floor.

Kara's whole body burned as he looked down at her breasts. Appreciation darkened his eyes to emerald glitter, and the low, intensely sexual catch in his breath told her all she needed to know. *He was over the line.*

He touched her; took the weight of her breasts in his hands, sliding his thumbs over her nipples, slipping his tongue into her mouth. His hands were hot, his mouth hotter, the skin of his back hotter still. Searing. Scorching. She stroked him everywhere, and he dipped her backwards again to lift her breasts to his waiting, hungry mouth. His hand slid inside her knickers to mould her backside as he mouthed her bullet-hard nipples, one then the other, again, and then again.

He lifted her off her feet as she straightened and she wrapped her legs around his waist, locking her ankles together behind his back. Dylan held her easily in his arms, kissing her senseless as his fingers explored the silk between her legs. He had her desperate, unable to breathe with wanting him to push the material aside and touch her properly.

"Let's take this inside, English." His voice cracked, raw and unsteady. "Let me take you to my bed." His fingers pushed the material a little deeper into her. "Let me take these off for you, and kiss you here," he thumbed her clitoris, making her moan.

"And Kara?" he breathed, sliding just the tip of one finger under the material. "The boots stay on."

Chapter Ten

Dylan jumped down onto the lower deck and turned to help Kara down after him, kissing her stomach as it slid past his lips, then lingering on her naked breasts because he couldn't help himself.

"Bedroom," she said, lifting his head to hers. "Now."

He led her by the hand into the boat and lifted the trapdoor to the bedroom.

She eyed it sceptically. "Really?"

He looked at her, naked apart from her boots and lace knickers, her hands on her hips. The coolest cowgirl in the world. If she produced a gun from those itty-bitty lace panties and shot him right in the heart now, he'd die a happy man.

"Really." He waved his arm in front of him towards the hatch. "You first, or me. You choose. Either way I can promise you that I won't look up your skirt."

"Cute, Sailor." Kara put her head on one side, studying the options. " You can go first and demonstrate."

Dylan turned and lowered himself down the hatch, proficient after the benefit of a few days' practice.

"Come down backwards, same as me. It's easiest."

Her boots appeared first, followed by smooth, brown calves. She stilled for a moment when he kissed the sweet spot at the back of her knee, his hands already on her thighs, halfway between steadying and stroking. She dropped a foot down onto the next step, bringing her backside level with his mouth.

He needed her to stop.

"Hold it there one second," he said, moulding her warm curves in his hands and letting his mouth drift over the strip of lace that covered next to nothing. She had skin like the velvet petals of a rose and the kick-ass attitude of the prickliest cactus, and it was turning out to be a combination that drove him crazy.

She was turned on. The subtle movement through her hips told him so. She was offering herself, opening herself to his mouth. He pulled her panties to the side and slid his fingers into the heat between her legs, loving the way she gasped and rocked her hips a little harder. Fuck, she was wet and ready, and his every instinct was to drop his jeans and screw her there and then against the stepladder.

He pressed his whole body against her legs, his mouth a breath away from her sex.

He didn't want to be a breath away. He wanted her spreadeagled on his bed.

He pushed a finger inside her, dipping his head between her legs to lick where he'd stroked, laughing low when she tried to open her legs further to encourage him in. She was so close to coming, but she was also close to breaking her neck. He didn't want her to break her neck, because he wanted to screw her until she forgot her own name.

He straightened and slipped his arms around her, finding her nipples and rolling them.

"Get your ass down off this ladder and into my bed, English."

She slithered down, a bundle of curves and flushed skin in the glow of the bedside light.

She paused for a second, her eyes flickering around the low, velvet-encased boudoir. He watched her, knowing what was going on in her head because he'd had that same reaction the first time he'd seen the place.

She turned to him, then stepped in close and ran her hand over his cock, flicking open the top button of his jeans.

She glanced at the low ceiling with a sigh of regret.

"I guess we'll have to save reverse cowgirl until another time," she murmured, flicking open his second button.

Dylan closed his eyes, but the image of Kara sitting astride his cock in just her cowboy boots stayed there anyway. His affection for the Love Tug waned rapidly with the realisation that it was never going to happen in this room, at least. She flicked a third button open and reached her hand inside, raising her eyebrows at the fact that he was naked beneath the denim.

"You thought I was a sure thing, Sailor?"

He shook his head. "Assumed nothing. Hoped some." He dragged in a deep breath as she dipped down onto her haunches to push his jeans off, her face level with his cock. He could feel the heat of her breath, and he groaned out loud when she licked him from base to tip, raising her eyes to his as she opened her mouth and took him inside.

If he lived another hundred years, he knew he'd never see anything as outright fucking beautiful.

He let her slide her mouth over him once more. Twice. And then he stopped her, because if she'd got to three, he wouldn't have had the self-control to stop her, and by four or five she'd have had him coming like a school boy.

He pulled her up to a standing position, kneading her behind as he kissed her. She tasted of him already.

"I want you underneath me the first time." He backed her towards the bed, pushing her panties down her thighs. "And I want to see your face when I make you come."

She sank down as the bed touched the back of her calves, and he bent to help her get the scrap of lace over her boots.

"I could just take my boots off," she offered.

Dylan shook his head and kissed her kneecap, tossing her panties aside. She was sitting on the edge of his bed, and she was naked. He parted her knees and knelt between them, rising up until he was eye to eye with her. Her mouth opened a little when he brushed the back of his fingers lightly over her sex, and he leaned in and kissed her.

"You like that?" he murmured, doing it again, letting his

fingers linger. Opening her, deliberate and slow.

Kara rested her forehead against his, her breathing short and shallow, her eyes glittering. She was waiting for more, and he had so much more he wanted to give her.

"So ready for me," he said, sliding the tips of his fingers over her, knowing full well that she needed more.

He groaned when her fingers curled around his shaft. She wasn't playing fair either.

"So ready for me," she whispered, and he turned his hand over and thrust two fingers inside her, loving the erotic sound of her moan.

"Dylan…"

His cock swelled harder at the sound of his name on her lips, making him reach for a condom from the drawer beside the bed.

She nodded, breathing hard, taking the foil packet from him and opening it with her teeth.

"Let me."

Protection had never been so sexy. She rolled it over his length with sure fingers, and he rewarded her by drawing delicate circles around her clitoris with his index finger as he traced her lips with his tongue. She kissed him back, her fingers twisting in his hair, her breath coming in short rasps.

"Lie back, English," he breathed, moving with her until they stretched out full length on the bed. She opened her thighs when he settled his body over hers, one thrust away from home. Her hand curved around his butt cheek, the other around the back of his neck.

It had to be now. He pushed his hips down, his breath leaving his chest in a rush as his cock thrust into the warmth and beauty of her body. Blood rushed to his brain. *Fuck. Fuck. Fuck.* Her fingernails dug into his ass where she gripped him, holding him deep inside her.

She opened her eyes when he smoothed her damp hair back from her face, and the trace of a smile crossed her kiss-swollen lips.

"I know," he said hoarsely, rocking his hips slowly over hers. "I know."

And then she wound those cowboy boots around his thighs, and all conscious thought left his head in favour of just feeling, and fucking.

Kara wrapped her legs tight around Dylan, hardly able to breathe around the need to come. He'd built her up to this from the moment she'd stepped aboard the boat, and every thrust of his cock edged her closer.

In the end, it wasn't his cock that made her orgasm. It was his words.

"I know."

He fucked her slowly, hard, and delicious, and when his hand snaked between their damp bodies to finger her clitoris, he said it again.

"I know, beautiful girl. I know."

Did he know? Did he feel it too, that this was the fuck of a lifetime? She was boneless, ready to come, wanting it to go on forever because she'd never known sex could be so all-encompassing. He touched her everywhere. Between her legs. Inside her head. Every inch of her body shimmered on the agonising, delicious edge of orgasm, then his tongue slid over hers as he started to thrust faster, spreading her wide with his knee against hers.

His fingers. His cock. His eyes. His mouth.

"Fuck, Kara, oh fuck…" His eyes locked with hers as her body bucked beneath him. He lost his control watching her face as she came beneath him, his body responding with hard slams that sent her orgasm spinning out all the way to her toes and fingertips.

She wrapped her arms around him and lifted her hips, dragging him deeper still, making him shudder with release as he came with her hips clamped tight against him. They fitted perfectly. A lock and a key.

They lay for a while afterwards, her fingers lazy over the contours of his back, his lips smooching the curve of her neck.

When she opened her eyes, the astral ceiling winked down at her. Sex-tired and content, a smile curved her lips as she smoothed a hand down the back of his head.

"You made me see stars, Sailor."

Chapter Eleven

"So how are we gonna play this thing, English?"

Kara accepted the steaming coffee mug Dylan held out and cradled it between her palms, still naked beneath the sheets of his ridiculously comfortable bed after a scant few hours of sleep. She leaned her head back against the padded headboard.

"Straight down the line," she said.

"I don't want to put you in a compromising position with Sophie and Lucien."

She shook her head. "You won't. They knew I was coming here last night."

"You told them?" He looked up from stepping out of his jeans, surprise in his clear green eyes.

"Of course." Kara shrugged. "Why not? I'm a big girl, they trust me to make my own decisions."

She didn't go into the fact that she and Sophie had sat down for a good hour yesterday evening talking it through, debating whether Kara was really ready to let someone close again after Richard's betrayal. Sophie and Lucien had scraped her up off the floor last summer and pieced her back together, a slightly more complicated puzzle than she'd been beforehand. She frowned a little, not appreciating thoughts of Richard intruding on her first Sunday morning wake-up with another man since their split.

Placing her coffee down, she let the sheet fall to her waist.

"Breakfast?" She smiled sweetly and raised her eyebrows.

Appreciation flared in Dylan's eyes as he sat down on the side of the bed. He tugged the sheet away, revealing her naked body to his greedy gaze.

"The full English, sir?" she said, letting him look his fill.

He moved closer to stroke her breasts. "You have a smart mouth."

"Do you like it?"

He snaked his tongue along her bottom lip. "I like it plenty." His hands tracked over her rib cage and settled on her hips. "I like all of you plenty."

His easy Californian accent softened his sensual words so that Kara found herself instinctively running her hands over the breadth of his shoulders, enjoying his body. "You're not so bad yourself, Sailor."

"In the interests of honesty, I feel I should tell you that I don't actually own this boat, and I've never sailed in my life."

Kara stroked her fingertips over his collarbones, unsure if she was relieved or disappointed that the Love Tug wasn't a direct reflection of Dylan's tastes.

"I'm still going to call you Sailor."

"Good. I like the way you say it."

"Sailor," she said, deliberately husky, letting her fingers trail down the definition of his stomach, enjoying the way his cock reacted with interest.

"Did you offer me breakfast?" he said, sliding his hand between her legs. "Because I've decided what I want."

"Hmm. What might that be?"

He opened her with his fingers, dropping his other hand down to explore her exposed sex.

"You." He kissed her shoulder. "This." He concentrated his attention on her clitoris, and she parted her legs wider for him. "Now."

Dylan bent over her body and placed butterfly trails of kisses over her inner thighs, then lay down on his side, rolling her onto hers too. He rested his head on her inner thigh when she lifted her knee, and gave a small sigh of appreciation when she mirrored the position, inverted between his thighs.

"I'm hungry too," she murmured, wrapping her arm over his hip, holding him close and loving the sight of his cock so close to her mouth. He was the most tempting breakfast she'd ever had before her.

He kept her waiting, letting her expectations heighten as he stroked the curves of her bottom and thighs, his lips everywhere but where she really wanted them to be. She repaid him in kind, massaging the firm cheeks of his ass, letting his cock brush her throat when she leaned in to lick the lines where his torso met his thigh.

And then he paused, splaying her sex wide with the fingertips of both his hands. Kara held her breath, her teeth grazing his inner thigh, waiting. He made her wait longer still, his fingertips massaging tiny circles where they pressed into her flesh.

"I'm not gonna rush this, English. I want you to remember it forever."

Was it possible to come just from being looked at, from anticipation and longing to be touched? Kara could feel Dylan's gaze heavy between her legs, and she thrilled at the heady, hard evidence of his arousal in front of her eyes. She cupped his balls, needing to touch him almost more than she needed him to touch her, gratified by the catch in his heated breath over her clitoris. She moaned out loud with giddy relief when his fingers finally slid over her, moaned louder still when the warmth of his open mouth lowered over her sex, his tongue and his fingers working his own unique brand of leisurely, sensual magic.

He took his time, and she wanted him to stay there forever.

Kara's hands explored his hardness, and she closed her eyes with pleasure when she took him into her mouth. Dylan's shuddering sigh of satisfaction vibrated from his tongue onto her clitoris, and she slid him in deeper as he screwed two fingers inside her.

They lay body to body, lost in the intimacy of giving and receiving. Of building and backing off, only to build again, a little higher each time. Kara's arm over his hip held him close, her fingers sliding over his butt cheeks, between them, pressing against the tightness there as the orgasm she'd tried to hold back flooded through her body like a tsunami. Surrendered. Euphoric. He clamped her against him, thrusting his cock into her mouth as she came against his relentless tongue. She read his fraught movements, knowing he was going to come, wanting to taste him when he did. He was granite-smooth and swollen in her mouth, and she gave him everything. Sliding her hands. Swirling her tongue. Tight, hot suction.

He wanted her to remember this forever.

She wanted him to never forget how she made him feel.

When she pressed her finger deeper between the firm cheeks of his ass, his hips jerked violently and his arm clamped her to him. He was gasping. Raw and laid bare, coming in her mouth and in her arms, his face pressed hard into her inner thigh.

Afterwards, Dylan twisted around and gathered Kara against him, his hand moving warm and languid over her breasts as their heartbeats slowed.

He reached up and traced his finger over the richly decorated ceiling, from planet earth across to the silver of the moon.

"To the moon and back, English."

Chapter Twelve

To: mollymk@toscanomail
From: mmk@toscanomail

Hey Mom,
Just checking in to make sure you're okay. How's Justin doing? Don't cover for him - if there's any trouble, you let me know, okay?
Remember I can be home within a day if you ever need me.
M x

To: mmk@toscanomail
From: mollymk@toscanomail

Stay where you are, son, Ibiza sounds like it's going to suit you.
You've done enough for your brother. More than anyone had any right to ask of you. Justin is… he's Justin, he'll never change.
I heard on the grapevine at Lorn's that Suzie is pregnant. Did you know?

Mom xx

Dylan stared at the screen for long minutes, the untouched cup of coffee in his hand going cold.

He could clearly picture his mother sitting under the dryer at Lorn's salon, her hair in rollers, reading some out of date magazine while the town's latest tittle-tattle flowed around her.

Her sons had provided a rich seam to mine for the local gossipmongers over the years, and she'd become accustomed to wearing her silence and serenity like an invisible cloak. It was that or fight back, and with sons like her boys, that was too much fighting for any one woman.

Suzie was pregnant. Dylan closed his laptop and looked out over the Mediterranean from the open fronted cafe, remembering his coffee and finding it unpalatably cold. *Was he bothered?* On some level, perhaps. He didn't want to analyse his own feelings where Suzie was concerned; she hadn't been his girl for a while now. They'd both moved on, through choice on her part and necessity on his. He'd filed her away, along with all of the other associated bad memories, in a seldom-visited box at the back of his brain. The box was dirty. Battered, as if it had been kicked around in a temper. Padlocked with a big rusty lock that he'd deliberately lost the key to because he never wanted to have to open it again.

This was home now. Ibiza. Sunshine. Sand. Sea. Sexy girls in cowboy boots.

He hadn't expected to find sanctuary on board a boat kitted out with its own private glitter-ball, or in the arms of a girl with wild curls and questionable taste in footwear. But then he'd learned the hard way that life throws you curveballs, and sometimes the best thing to do is just try and catch them, hoping like hell that no one guesses you don't even know the rules of the game.

Chapter Thirteen

Sophie turned off the webcam, tears on her cheeks from blowing kisses to Tilly and her parents after their daily catch up session. Being apart from their daughter was proving hard on her heart, even if she was clearly having the time of her little life being spoiled rotten by her grandparents.

Lucien handed her a chilled glass of wine and stroked a tender hand down her hair.

"Don't cry on your birthday, Princess. She'll be here next week."

Sophie placed her hand over his on her shoulder and turned to kiss his knuckles, knowing that Lucien missed their little girl almost as much as she did.

"Being here alone has its compensations," he murmured, taking her hand and tugging her to her feet. "Come with me. I made dinner reservations."

"You did?"

He rolled his eyes. "Come with me."

Sophie let him lead her, her eyes drawn as always to the lone wolf inked across his naked, sun bronzed back, brought to life by the subtle shift of his muscles as he moved. At thirty-six, he was a man who turned the heads of women in any room he walked into, yet whose own head was turned by no one but her. His loyalty and lust were for Sophie alone, a thrill that never got old for her.

"I need to go and get ready," Sophie said veering off towards the stairs down to their suite.

"No you don't."

Lucien didn't turn around, just kept hold of her hand and led her out onto the terrace and down the warm stone steps at the side of the villa. Heady, scented honeysuckle meandered along the wall beside them, loading the air with sweetness as anticipation warmed Sophie's bones. Lucien had assumed an air of mystery, which usually meant nothing but good things. Sometimes wild things, sometimes shocking things, but always, always good.

He turned to her at the bottom of the steps, reaching into his jeans pocket and producing a large, old key. "This way." He slid the key into an arched gate in the wall, then shouldered it open. Sophie glanced past him to see what lay beyond. She hadn't ventured past that point, in truth she hadn't given any thought to what was on the other side of the gate. Cliff, she'd vaguely assumed.

Lucien stepped through and set off down the rocky, uneven path, Sophie following close behind him.

"What's down here?"

"Dinner."

She glanced dubiously around the small slice of wilderness. "Do we have to catch it with our bare hands?"

"Would I make you do that on your birthday?"

He wouldn't, she was almost certain. *Almost.* Previous birthdays had involved many things: surprise trips, private movie screenings, jewels that had made her gasp. This was a different approach, very different. Picking her way down a dusty Ibizan cliffside like a mountain goat was definitely unusual.

"Nearly there," he said, then turned unexpectedly and drew her against him for a slow, sizzling kiss. For a few seconds Sophie didn't give the slightest thought to where they were heading, because being kissed by Lucien was utterly immersive. His hand drifted over her breast, and she felt her nipple ripen for him through her flimsy sundress.

"You're not wearing a bra," he murmured, drawing his thumb

around the nipple.

"No."

He ran an experimental hand down her spine and over her backside, checking if she had anything at all on beneath the cotton. She didn't. She gasped when he unexpectedly lifted the dress up, grasping the seams as he tugged it off over her head.

"Lucien," she breathed, feeling exposed and instantly hot for him.

"If it was up to me you'd never wear clothes," he said, his hands back on her breasts as his tongue moved lazily in her mouth. He stopped when she slid her hands down his abs and popped the top button on his jeans.

"Not me, Princess. Just you."

He stepped away from her and inclined his head towards where the path ahead of them curved out of sight.

"Dinner is just around the corner."

Panic warmed Sophie's cheeks. "I'm not going to find a table full of people round there, am I?" She'd taken Kara at face value when she'd said that she was spending the night with Dylan. Had she been covering for Lucien's birthday surprise?

He glanced back to her. "Now why didn't I think of that?"

"Because you know I'd die of embarrassment?"

He must have caught the genuine anxiety in her voice, because he stopped and turned again, his palm soft against her hair.

"Just us, Princess. I promise." He traced a fingertip from her lips, between her breasts, over her stomach, and came to rest just above the crevice between her legs. "No one else gets to see you like this."

The possessive edge to his softly spoken words served only to make them sexier. He was a caveman in all the best ways. He moved his finger inside her folds for the most fleeting of seconds, his eyes knowing on hers as he skimmed her clitoris before turning his back to lead her on to dinner.

She came to an abrupt standstill when they rounded the rock, completely taken by surprise at what she saw.

"I never even realised this was here," she said, her palm flat against her breastbone.

"I know. I wanted to keep it a surprise."

She stepped forwards into a natural, totally private alcove worn into the rock, so deep it made a room in itself, enclosed by its three rocky walls. A four-poster day-bed nestled in the space, made of simple plain driftwood dressed with gauzy white drapes and sheets. Beyond the alcove, the cliff dropped away down to the sea below. In the distance the huge peach sun sank slowly into the horizon. Candles flickered on the natural ledges around the alcove, and a table stood beside the bed topped with silver domes. For a few seconds Sophie forgot she was naked. Lucien's birthday surprise had completely enchanted her.

And then he moved in close and dropped to his knees in front of her, and she remembered again, really fast.

"So, it's your birthday," he said, wrapping his arms around her thighs and kissing her stomach. Her shoulders touched the smooth, cool stone wall behind her as Lucien hooked her leg over his shoulder, opening her sex to his eyes. He cradled the cheeks of her ass in his hands and looked up her body. "Let me give you something."

His eyes were hot, never leaving hers as he tipped his face up and opened his mouth over her. He loved doing this. He'd told her often, so many times when his head had been buried between her legs just as it was now.

Sophie moaned, instinctively stroking a hand over his hair as he went to work on her, probing her delicate folds, using his fingers to expose her clitoris to his waiting tongue. He knew her body so intimately, knew how suckling her right there built her orgasm like quicksilver. He suckled her then, swirling his tongue over her nub as his hands massaged her backside. She didn't try to hold her orgasm back as her body started its delicious tremble. Life with Lucien had taught her that her next orgasm was never far away... and it was her birthday, after all.

He read her signs and swirled harder, tighter, fast little circles that made her hips rock into his face. He answered by lifting her against his mouth and clamping her there, giving her so much stimulation that her orgasm erupted through her body like a firework, spangling every nerve ending with hot glitter. He loved her through it with his mouth and his hands, and when it was over he lowered her down onto her knees and gathered her into him.

Sophie wound her arms around him, clinging to his strength, and his warmth. "I love you," she mouthed against his shoulder, feeling him say it back against her hair. And she did, she really did. He was the owner of her heart, the father of her child. They shared everything.

Except for one final thing. A thing she mostly tried not to think about. But the moment was too perfect. She was brave enough. She would say it today. She looked up at him, connecting with his gaze, her eyes steady and intimate.

"You know what I'd really like for my birthday, Lucien?"

"Anything," he murmured, and she knew that he meant it. He'd move mountains to give her what she wanted. She paused for a few seconds, but her eyes didn't waver.

"I want to be your wife."

She felt him still. It was the only thing that they didn't talk about. When she'd met Lucien, she'd been unhappily married to someone else and his opinion on matrimony was in the gutter. So much had happened over the intervening years to heal both of their wounds, yet still it was not an easy subject to raise. It was their last taboo.

Lucien reached for her hand and moved it between their bodies until it settled over his heart. "I'm already yours, in here."

"I know that," she said, easing back to look him in the eyes again.

"Then why?" It wasn't a confrontational question, more of a genuine need to know. Marriage just wasn't Lucien's idea of an expression of love.

Sophie placed her hand on his cheek. Her man. Her beautiful,

beautiful man.

"Because I want to be your wife. I want to take your name. I want to wear your ring. I want to call you my husband."

She watched his eyes as she spoke, saw them soften with each new declaration.

"I don't care where, or when, or who else is there, Lucien. I don't need a big party or a flashy diamond." Sophie's voice cracked. "I just want to marry you."

Lucien looked at the woman he loved, kneeling before him on her birthday, asking to become his wife. He'd always known that marriage held more relevance for Sophie than for him, but hearing her say that she wanted to take his name, to wear his ring… it stirred feelings in him that he didn't even know he possessed. He *hadn't* possessed them before Sophie. 'I want to be your wife,' she'd said, catching him unawares, as ever the girl who surprised him.

"Stand up, Princess."

A flicker of apprehension crossed her brow as she took his hand to steady herself as she stood.

That was better. His girl wanted to be his wife, and she was going to get the proposal she deserved. She was not the one who should be on her knees.

"I'm not down on one knee, Sophie. I'm on both." He held her hands, and could feel them shaking. "I'm kneeling because you humble me. I'm kneeling because you light up my life from the inside out. I'm kneeling because you're the most fucking beautiful woman in this whole world, and an amazing mother to our amazing child. You're the love of my lifetime."

She gripped his fingers hard, damp cheeked and shiny eyed in the candlelight.

"Every now and then I forget how spectacular you are, Sophie." He brought her hand to his mouth and kissed it, her skin warm, her scent familiar beneath his lips. "You just reminded me."

And then he said the words that he'd never once imagined he'd say.

"Marry me. Please?"

Chapter Fourteen

"Oh my God!" Kara shot off her stool, her cereal forgotten as she scooted around the breakfast bar to hug Sophie, almost lifting her off her feet in her delight. "What took you so long, Mr. K?" she laughed, turning to kiss Lucien on the cheek too.

"Who said I did the asking?" he said, lifting his eyebrows as he slithered off his stool and picked up his car keys. Sophie brushed toast crumbs from her hands and put her arms around his neck as he leaned in close to kiss her goodbye.

"We both did the asking," she murmured, smiling as his lips touched hers. He tasted of fresh coffee and of lazy weekend mornings in bed, and she suddenly wished they were back there right now. His hand massaged her hip for a few seconds when she held him close and let her tongue flick against his, lingering. His low sigh told her he appreciated her giving him more than he'd expected.

She smiled softly when he lifted his head.

"I think you're going to like having me as your wife." She ran her thumb over his bottom lip then let him go with a gentle push. "Go to work. We'll be in soon."

Lucien straightened reluctantly, tugging Kara's ponytail as he passed her on the way out of the kitchen.

"Don't fill Sophie's head with crazy wedding plans," he said, knowing full well that she was going to.

"So. Tell me everything," Kara poured them both a fresh mug of coffee and sat down again opposite Sophie. "When, where, how. I need details." She sipped her drink. "Unless you were actually shagging and he yelled it when he blew his load, in which case feel free to lie."

Sophie grinned. Kara's directness always amused her.

"Okay… we were in the secret alcove at the bottom of the garden…"

"What alcove?"

"It's… well, it's kind of a secret… like an outdoor bedroom in the cliff."

"Whoa!" Kara held up her hand, banging her mug down on the breakfast bar. "We have a secret sex alcove at the bottom of the garden?"

"Who knew? I was as surprised as you," Sophie said mildly. "Anyway, I said that what I'd really like for my birthday was a husband, so he got down on his knees and asked me to marry him."

Kara shook her head. "Wow. I don't think there's another person in this world who that man would get on his knees for."

They paused in silence for a second, then both spoke at the same time.

"Tilly."

It was true. The tiny child had her daddy wrapped around her chubby little finger.

"She is going to be the most adorable flower girl," Kara said, reaching out and covering Sophie's hand with her own.

Sophie nodded, damp-eyed. "With you to look after her as my maid of honour?"

It was Kara's turn to well up, and she reached for a nearby box of tissues and dragged them over.

"What are we like?" She laughed shakily. "I think we can safely assume that your wedding day will not turn into the fiasco that mine did. Lucien adores you."

"I know he does." Sophie grabbed a tissue too. "I thought it might be nice to have the wedding in Norway."

Kara slid her mug across the counter and touched it against Sophie's in assent.

"God, yes! I'd love that. Maybe I can snag myself a Viking of my own after all."

"If you still need to. You seem pretty loved up with a certain American hottie right now."

"Sexed up, not loved up," Kara corrected.

"One has a habit of leading to the other," Sophie said.

"Not for this gal," Kara said, sliding off her stool. "I'm happy for sex to just lead to more sex right now."

"I know... but he seems like a nice guy, that's all."

Kara picked up the keys to the Mustang. "As did Richard this time last year. And we all know how that one turned out, don't we?"

She prepared herself for the usual stabbing sensation that she always felt when she said his name. Whether it was pain from her own heart or the desire to stab his she wasn't entirely certain, but either way, it didn't come.

Fuck, she'd finally done it. She'd moved on. Washed that man right out of her hair. Richard had made the coward's choice on their wedding day, having been issued an ultimatum by his surreptitious girlfriend. Standing at the altar in the ivory dress of her dreams and waiting for a man who didn't show had been the most humiliating experience of her life, and it had taken a lot of tears and bottles of vodka to set her on the road to recovery.

And now, finally, it would appear that she had arrived. She stood stock still, her hand over her heart and her eyebrows raised towards her best friend.

"Well, what do you know? I was right all along. The best way to get over a man *is* to get under another one." She sashayed out of the kitchen, elated.

At the club later that afternoon, Dylan rocked back in his swivel chair and stretched his arms above his head. Lucien sat alongside him and rolled his shoulders as he closed computer files down, work done at last for the day. Opening night was drawing closer and they'd spent the afternoon going over fine details to make sure that everything was in place to guarantee a seamless launch. The press were hungry to see how the club fared on the famed White Isle. While Lucien refused to hide their raison d'etre beneath a veil of prudishness, he equally didn't allow his clubs to be categorised as seedy. They were hedonist palaces of intense pleasure for the open minded, and he was fiercely proud of the empire he'd created. The impression that the first night would create on guests and the media mattered to him very much.

He opened the desk door and placed a bottle of whisky and two glasses on the top. "Drink?"

"Sure," Dylan said, watching Lucien pour out two heavy-handed measures. He'd come to admire the other man's business acumen over the couple of weeks they'd worked together, and sensed that he was someone who played it straight down the line. Dylan was gratified that their business relationship was definitely moving into the territory of friendship too. He really liked this guy.

Lucien took a conversational tone.

"I asked Sophie to marry me yesterday."

Dylan grinned and accepted the glass Lucien held out along with the confidence he'd shared.

"No way, man! Congratulations!" The whisky hit his throat with a welcome burn. "Although… I'd kind of assumed that you guys were married anyway."

Lucien knocked back a good slug of whisky. "It's never been high on our list."

Dylan nodded slowly, his mind back in the States. "I know what you mean." He regretted his choice of words as soon as they were out, and Lucien was too clever by far to miss the fact that his response was laden with meaning.

"You do?"

Measured words were needed. "I've been close once or twice," he said non-committally, draining his glass then scrubbing his hand over the roughness of his cheek with a half smile.

"Women, huh?" He was well aware that his sweeping generalisation sounded lame.

Lucien lifted one shoulder as he replenished their glasses.

"Dylan, I'll be straight with you. I offered you this job on instinct, and you haven't given me cause to regret it. You obviously know your way around this business."

Relieved that the conversation had changed course, Dylan relaxed.

"I'm excited about it. This whole island sits well with me, the job too. It feels good."

"Should I have asked you for references? Would you, if you were me?"

Okay, not so relaxed. He shrugged, his expression turning philosophical.

"I appreciate that you didn't. In all honesty, I wouldn't have found it easy to provide them."

Lucien eyed him steadily, waiting for more. They were similar in age, equals in body and in strength of mind. Dylan came from a family where brotherhood had turned out to stand for very little, yet he felt a quiet unity and trust in Lucien Knight.

He didn't want to lie to this man. He just wanted a clean slate and a simple life.

"Things didn't go well for me back home." He sighed heavily and took a deep slug of whisky. "I left with nothing but the shirt on my back, and none of that shit will follow me here." He shook his head, the memories all ugly. "Trust me, I'd've been happy to never set foot on American soil again if it wasn't for my mom."

A look of understanding passed between the two men. Dylan didn't know it, but he'd managed to say the one thing that reassured Lucien most.

"So, this thing you've got going on with Kara…" Lucien said, changing the conversational course once more and leaving his sentence there for Dylan to make of it whatever he wanted.

A slow smile crept across Dylan's face at the mention of her name.

"She's a breath of fresh air."

"She's not as tough as she makes out."

For all her smart one-liners and her bold moves, Dylan had seen the fragility behind Kara's eyes. "I get that."

It was the thing that scared him most about her.

"Kara's history is hers to share, but you should know she's the closest thing I have to a sister."

Lucien's message could not have been clearer, and Dylan admired him all the more for his loyalty.

"I'll never hurt her on purpose."

"It's easily done."

Dylan swirled the whisky in his glass. "I get that too."

His heart felt oddly heavy in his chest long after the conversation had ended. He'd forgotten that feeling in the last few weeks, but now it was back with him. *Could he really have this life? Was he entitled to it, after all that had gone before?* He badly needed to believe that the answer was yes.

Chapter Fifteen

"Throwing yourself a party, Sailor?" Kara sat down at the bar a couple of evenings later, the bangles around her wrist clattering against the mirrored surface. Dylan was working late again, the mellow sound of Bob Marley low in the background as he studied an array of rainbow coloured liqueurs and bottles of spirits lined up across the bar. Sophie and Lucien had left together an hour or two before, leaving Kara and Dylan behind to lock up.

"Every club needs its signature cocktail."

"It does?" Kara turned the closest bottle towards her, reading the label on the deep amber liquid. "Hierbas?"

Dylan nodded.

"Top of the list. It's locally made." He took the bottle from her and opened it. "The taste of Ibiza." He held it out for her to smell. She inhaled, catching notes of fresh lavender and herbs.

"It smells like summer," she said as Dylan reached for a shot glass and poured out a little for her to try. The flavours burst in her mouth: sweet aniseed, fragrant herbs, and smooth, warm alcohol. "Wow," she laughed. "That's... potent."

"Yes it is," Dylan murmured, setting the bottle to one side and opening a bottle of Cava from the fridge.

"This is turning into my kind of Friday night," Kara said, as Dylan reached down a champagne flute from the overhead rack and poured her a glass. She watched him as he studied the bottles on the bar, selecting the odd one and either shortlisting it next to the Hierbas or else putting it back in its place behind him on the shelf.

"You've done this before, huh?"

He shrugged. "Some."

"Can you toss the shaker behind your back? Please say yes," Kara giggled, halfway towards a Tom Cruise fantasy already.

Dylan rolled his eyes. He'd cut his teeth on all that stuff, it was second nature.

"For sure. But I'm not doing it for you now."

"You so are," Kara placed her Cava down. "I'd like a Sex on the Beach, please barman, followed by a Slow Comfortable Screw."

Dylan shook his head, the trace of a laugh on his face.

"Predictable." He measured Hierbas into a glass cup and then into a silver beaker.

"A Screaming Orgasm then?" She tilted her head to one side winsomely and batted her eyelashes. "Please?" Just saying the words warmed the pit of her stomach, because Dylan Day was capable of exactly that with just a few flicks of his fingers. It was verging on embarrassing how easily the man could make her come.

He lifted his amused eyes to hers, and then reached for a mortar and pestle. She sat for a few seconds as he plucked fresh mint from a plant on the back of the bar then set to work. She watched his hands, the slow grinding motion as he crushed the leaves. She wanted them on her instead.

Reaching behind her neck, she pulled the ties of her halter necked sundress open and let it fall to her waist.

Dylan ran his tongue over his lips. He paused, then seemed to think better of it and continued to add a little Cava to the crushed mint.

Kara unclipped her strapless bra and peeled it from her body, holding it up for a second and letting it fall fluidly from her fingertips. She didn't need to look down to know that her nipples were hard. Her body was screaming for him.

"Slippery Nipple?" she said, her eyes on his as she slid her hands over herself, tweaking her nipples lightly for his benefit. She had him and she knew it. His eyes darkened. He set the cocktail equipment down to one side and walked slowly round to her side of the bar.

Swinging her stool around to face him, he opened her knees and moved to stand between them.

"I think I'd better test that claim, English," he said, and Kara sighed into his mouth as it covered hers at the same time as his hands covered her breasts. He rolled her nipples slowly, his tongue sliding over hers.

"You lied," he murmured. "Not slippery."

He reached for the bottle of Hierbas and tipped a little into his mouth, then lowered his head and closed his mouth over her nipple. His hands spanned her ribcage above her pushed down dress, holding her steady as he kissed his way over her curves to give her other breast some attention. Heat, and the slide of his tongue around her sensitive nipple, then delicious suction.

"Now they're slippery," he said as he raised his head. "Slippery, and sexy, and delicious."

His mouth tasted of warm, sweet summer sunshine when he kissed her again, a sensual assault, his hands sliding into her hair.

"If I fucked you right now, would you be slippery there too?" he breathed, pressing the hardness of his cock into the silk of her knickers below her rucked up skirt. Just as Kara decided that Hierbas was her favourite drink in the whole wide world, he pulled back, dropped a kiss that lingered on the hollow at the base of her neck, and then returned to the other side of the bar.

She stared at him, her breath coming in less than regular gasps.

"I'm working," he said, steadily. "And you're a beautiful distraction."

He strained the mint infusion into the Hierbas in the metal shaker. His eyes ran over the coloured spirits in front of him.

"Which one, English?" he said. "Which one would you choose?"

Did he actually expect her to have a lucid opinion on anything other than how much she wanted him to get naked? In the background, Bob Marley helpfully suggested she should stir it up as she scanned the bottles quickly.

"The blue one," she said, at random.

He frowned thoughtfully, then shrugged and picked the blue curacao out of the line up. Lurid as it was, its bitter orange flavour might just harmonise well. He measured it out and added it to the mint and Hierbas in the shaker.

Kara crossed her legs and picked up the glass of Cava he'd just topped up for her, learning patience, now beginning to enjoy his slow game because she was pretty certain that it would end with what she so much wanted. She held out a cautionary hand as he screwed the top onto the cocktail shaker and hefted it.

"Take your shirt off before you do that."

"Before I shake the cocktail?"

"You heard me, Sailor."

He sighed for effect, but she didn't mistake it for genuine boredom because his eyes told her how hot he was for her. He was as into this as she was.

She pulled her bottom lip between her teeth and held it there as his fingers worked the buttons on his shirt open, revealing inch on inch of golden goodness. His shoulders gleamed as he rolled them to shrug the shirt off and dropped it.

"Better?" He lifted his hands to the side, palms up.

She slowly released her lip, now plumped from having been bitten, and watched his eyes follow the movement, with satisfaction.

"For now." She sipped her wine. "Now, toss things."

He looked away, shaking his head, half laughing.

"I don't do this stuff anymore," he protested, picking up a bottle of neon yellow liqueur by the neck and flicking it in a graceful arch over his head. Kara watched, wide-eyed, as it somersaulted a couple of times then landed neatly in his other hand. She clapped with delight.

"Wow!" The display of his body moving under the bar's

spotlights and the way he made his showmanship look so easy was thoroughly intoxicating.

"Topless barmen. Write that down for your next business meeting with Lucien." She rolled her gaze deliberately over his body. "A winner every single time."

"Sexist, English. So sexist," he chided.

She shrugged, not in the least bit sorry.

"Now, make me a cocktail. Something sexy."

She sat back, unselfconscious with her body on display. He was in her thrall and he knew it. He studied her for a few seconds, and then seemed to make his decision. He turned his back on her, and she caught her breath, admiring him all over again. He was a man at home in his skin, from his lithe, sun-kissed shoulders to the lickable dip at the base of his spine revealed by the jeans slung low on his hips. Tawny lights gleamed in his hair when he moved, stretching for a bottle. There was a grace and a strength to the man that stopped her breath for a few seconds.

And then he tossed a cocktail shaker over his shoulder and caught it as he turned about, flipping a bottle from the bar so a little of its peachy nectar went into the shaker. Rum flew overhead next, the bottle spiralling into his hand to be tipped into the shaker too. It was like a well-rehearsed circus act, as natural as walking the tightrope for the acrobat. Bottles rolled from his wrist to his shoulder and back into his hand again in a blink, ice cubes jumped one, two three in the air before hitting the tumbler. And then he was done, screwing the lid on before shaking the concoction high then low. He slid a glass along the bar and tipped the cocktail out with a final flourish, crushed ice suspended in glittering golden liquid.

"One Naked Lady."

Kara gave him another burst of applause, her eyes round with delight. His hand caught hers as she reached for the glass.

"Not until you're a naked lady too."

She paused for a heartbeat, then kicked off her shoes and

shimmied down from the stool. Her dress didn't take much encouraging to fall down her hips, leaving her standing in the briefest scrap of midnight blue silk.

"I'm afraid I'm going to have to insist on full nudity, lady. House rules," he said, his fingers still around her glass. The gravelly edge to his voice told her that he appreciated what he saw.

"I really *do* want to taste that drink," she murmured, running one finger inside the top edge of the silk.

"I *really* want you to taste it," he said. "Take your panties off, English. Be naked for me."

Kara glanced behind her at the deserted dance floor, at the luxurious booths set around it which would very soon be filled with pleasure seekers. She was completely certain that no matter what happened in this place after opening night, no one would feel more filled to the brim with boiling, molten lust that she did at that exact moment. She burned with it. Burned for him.

Walking around the bar to where he stood watching her, she paused close to him and brushed her hand down the centre of his body, lower to give his crotch a light massage, then sashayed past him to run her hand over the elegant supportive column that rose from the bar to the ceiling. Covered in tiny mirrored tiles that reflected the colours and lights around it, it created a sparkling, soaring cascade of light when the club was in full flow. The bar beyond it wasn't stocked yet, and the surface was clear. *Perfect.*

Using a nearby upturned crate as a step, she hopped up onto the bar and leaned her back against the glittering column. Dylan picked up the cocktail he'd made for her and walked slowly towards her as she stepped delicately out of her knickers and slid down to sit on the bar, one leg stretched out in front of her, the other bent to rest her elbow on. She cupped her chin and smiled artfully.

"Do I get my drink now?"

Wordlessly he passed her the glass, his eyes moving over her body. He chose the moment she raised the glass to her lips to glide his hand down the outside of her raised thigh, moving beneath to stroke between her legs as the drink filled her mouth.

"What can you taste, English?"

"Apricots." *Touch me.* "Lemon." *Open me.* "Rum." *Fuck me.*

"Very good," he murmured, kissing her kneecap then lowering it towards him on the bar, opening her legs.

"Anything else?" he whispered, mouthing her nipple as his fingers moved inside her folds.

All she could think of was the heat. In her mouth and between her legs.

"Warm," she said, taking a little more into her mouth and leaning her head back against the pillar, arching her back with pleasure when Dylan pushed his fingers inside her.

"So warm," he said, his breath hot against her ear. "So warm, and wet, and open."

His low, sexy drawl sent long, delicious shivers through her body.

"Say something else," she said. "Keep talking."

Kara felt the curve of his smile as his tongue traced her earlobe.

"You like dirty talk, English?" The involuntary yelp that left her body was confirmation enough for both of them. "You want me to tell you how good it feels to spread your legs wide open and fuck you with my fingers?" He crooked his fingers inside her, finding her g-spot and massaging it. "You want me to tell you how much I love watching your mouth when you're excited, and feeling your clit swell when I touch it? How much I want to lick it right now?" He used his thumb to demonstrate, the pad of it flat on her clitoris, massaging. "To taste you, to feel you come in my mouth?"

He had her so high she could almost see stars. "Or maybe you want me to tell you how hard my cock is for you, and how it's actually fucking hurting me because I want to screw you so badly? Is that it, Kara?"

He had a way of only using her name at the very best moments, and she instinctively reached down and covered him with her hand, kneading him. The feel of him rigid beneath her fingers excited her almost beyond reason.

"You see how hard you've got me?" he said, sliding her closer and lifting her off the bar with one arm as he unbuttoned his jeans.

He turned her and bent her over the bar. The tear of foil was music to her ears, and seconds later he was against her, rocking his cock along the length of her sex. The mirrored surface of the bar chilled her nipples, and Dylan was oh so hot between her thighs.

And then he was inside her, hard and thick, making her gasp his name and look for something to hold onto.

His hand lay splayed between her shoulder blades, pinning her down as he thrust into her. Hard. She wanted harder still.

"More," she gasped. "More."

He paused, then moved back a fraction and lowered them both down until her knees felt the cool, hard floor behind the bar.

"Like this?" he ground out, throwing his hips forward so his cock hit home again and again. He wound her hair around his hand when she dropped her head back. "Will you come if I touch your clit now, English?"

She was pretty sure she was going to come just at the sound of his rasped words. Her stomach muscles jumped when he slid his hand over them, gliding down between her spread legs.

Greedy for him, she spread her knees wider, and he responded with an intensely sexual, guttural moan. His steady, hard thrusts pounded faster, harder, and she met him slam for slam, taking him to the hilt, trembling as her orgasm happened beneath his fingers and around his cock.

"Fuck," he gasped, his body juddering behind her once, twice, and then again before he finally slowed.

Dylan crouched over her, pulling her down with him when he

collapsed sideways onto the bar floor. He surrounded her, his heart beating hard against her back, every bit as erratically as her own.

Bob Marley crooned in the background. *Is this love*, he asked? 'No,' Kara replied in her head, euphoric, dreamy. 'It's not love, but it sure as hell is the best sex ever.'

Dylan wrapped himself around the warmth and softness of Kara's body, filling his hands and his mind with her to keep it from all of the bad stuff. Bob Marley suggested putting his cards on the table, as he closed his eyes and inhaled the scent of her.

No way. No fucking way.

Chapter Sixteen

Blissful didn't cover Sophie's joy when Tilly and her nanny arrived in Ibiza the following weekend. The little girl shattered the peaceful vibe of the villa into a million pieces, much to the satisfaction of her daddy. Sophie watched them from the kitchen window, Lucien lifting a shrieking Tilly over his head in the swimming pool, that big baby laugh shaking her entire body when he splashed her down again into the water.

Of all of the changes she'd witnessed in him over the years, the way he'd embraced fatherhood had been the most profound. To the rest of the world he was still the charismatic, uber-glamorous poster boy of the adult entertainment industry; it was only within the confines of their home that he relaxed his guard. Sophie alone knew his intricacies, the fears that drove him and kept him strong.

He was a different man in many ways these days. He'd turned the hot glare of danger to a lower simmer; the heat was still there, but quietened by the safety of being loved. In other ways he'd become stronger still. He was a warrior for his family, their strength and their protector.

She watched him climb out of the water with Tilly on his shoulders, her sweet limbs wrapped around the lone wolf tattoo inked over his shoulders. Sophie knew it by heart. She'd traced her fingers over it countless times, reminded each time of his heritage, his dark days, and gladdened that Lucien was no longer lonely.

"I think I've tired her out." Lucien walked inside a couple of minutes later, the sleepy child, wrapped in a towelling robe, resting on his shoulder. Tilly's flopped arm and relaxed fingers told Sophie she was already snoozing, and a peep over Lucien's shoulder confirmed it.

"I'll put her down if you like," Kara offered, walking in from poolside and pushing her sunglasses up on top of her head. She wasn't a woman who went mushy at the sight of a baby, yet something about Tilly had got under her skin. They seemed to connect, probably because Tilly was showing signs of being every bit as precocious as her mother's best friend.

Lucien dropped on the sofa as Kara left the room with Tilly in her arms, and Sophie flopped beside him. The sun had dried the pool water from his skin, leaving him warm to the touch and smelling of holidays and good times. She looped her arm over his bare midriff and snuggled into him, grabbing the moment to be alone.

"I've been thinking about the wedding…" she said, enjoying the weight of the arm Lucien slung across her shoulders.

"And?" he said, rubbing the top of her arm.

"I thought Norway?"

He turned his head and looked down at her, thoughtful. "I thought here."

"Here? In Ibiza?" Sophie said, surprised.

He nodded. "At the end of the summer."

"As in… the next couple of months?" she said, even more surprised. They hadn't talked about timescales, she'd just assumed that it would be some time the following year.

"Just you, me, and Tilly."

Sophie paused, struck by the romantic image of the three of them in the sunshine, daisies in Tilly's hair.

"We'd need witnesses, at least," she said, uncertain if she loved his idea or not.

"Kara and Dylan," Lucien said, slotting the pieces into place. "I'd like to take you home to London as Mrs. Knight," he smooched the sensitive skin below her ear. It was the first time he'd ever said the words 'Mrs. Knight,' and a slow zing of happiness spread a smile across her face.

The more she imagined it, the more she loved his plan.

"Okay," she said, laughing, turning into his kiss. "Okay. Ibiza it is. And soon."

The next couple of weeks slipped by with alarming speed, each day a day closer to launch night at the club. Kara's heart flipped whenever she drove past one of the huge, sexy roadside hoardings for Gateway Ibiza. VIP guests were invited, a celebrity DJ had signed on for a residency, and the press would be out in force. Lucien's PR machine had swung into full assault; there couldn't be many people on the island who didn't know they were there.

With twenty-four hours left to go, they were ready. Kara had spent her days over the last fortnight almost continually at the club, and her nights in bed with Dylan aboard the Love Tug. Her body ached pleasurably from being used in every way possible, and from using him right back. Had it really only been a few weeks since she'd first laid eyes on him? It felt much longer as the essence of him seeped under her skin, into her bones. He made her laugh, he made her moan, and he made her scream.

He made her happy.

To: mollymk@toscanomail
From: mmk@toscanomail

Hey mom,
Thinking about you, be strong. Billy wouldn't want you cry today, okay? It's launch night here for the new club, I'll raise a beer to him tonight.
M x

To: mmk@toscanomail
From: mollymk@toscanomail

I'm not sleeping son, I was just looking through some old photographs of you boys. I doubt your brother will even register the date. Three years without Billy already. It feels like so much longer.

Hope your day goes well. I rest easier knowing that you're out of it.

Mom xx

Dylan pushed his mobile into the pocket of his jeans, hating the image of his mom sitting alone late at night going through photos of her children in happier times. Scabbed knees and awful haircuts aplenty, no doubt, Billy always the joker with the biggest smile in the room.

Familiar, unsettling pain jostled his heart at the thought of Billy, his older brother by two years and his best friend as they grew up. He scrubbed his hands over his face harshly, trying to erase his melancholy mood. He owed it to Lucien to give this day his all. He was more than aware that without this job he'd most likely have had to move on weeks ago to someplace else, with no clear plan in mind. Drifting didn't suit him. He'd grown up in the heart of a big, bustling family; he wasn't accustomed to being cut adrift. Somehow he'd fallen on his feet here, into a job that consumed him, with people who invited him to bask in the warmth of their family.

And then there was Kara. Everything about the girl was pure gold, and every day the seeds of fear embedded themselves deeper into his gut. He was letting her invest her feelings, and he was investing his own, but it was all built on a house of cards. One push, and it would all fall in. Bitter experience had taught him that he could live through pretty much anything, but now, when it came to Kara, he wasn't so sure. If he was any kind of man he'd call a halt to it, but she had him enthralled. His brain said back off, but the rest of his body refused to listen. His cock stirred at the scent of her, and his mood lifted whenever she was near.

When it came to Kara Brookes, he feared he was a very selfish man.

Chapter Seventeen

The staff had all been on site since just after five, and Kara's entire body vibrated with first night nerves. This was by no means her first opening night, but that knowledge did nothing to slow the flood of adrenalin through her veins. She lived for nights like this - the thrills, the anticipation, the risk.

Not that there was much risk, really. Lucien and Dylan had made sure of that where the club was concerned, and she and Sophie were one hundred percent ready for curtain up in the boutique.

She looked slowly around, a careful three hundred and sixty degree spin. Every shelf stocked, every cabinet artfully lit, every mannequin unsuitably dressed. It looked beautiful; an elegant boudoir, a sexy prelude to the main event.

Over the past few years she'd become accustomed to the adult club scene, grown to love it even. She'd never been inside one as a paying customer. She wasn't sure she would have ever been brave enough, yet the idea of working here alongside Dylan over the summer made her body thrum with lust. Not that they could or would take part in the front of house action, but every time she looked at the bar she could only think of being bent over it by Dylan.

Launch night. The calm before the storm. She closed her eyes and breathed deeply. This was no mean feat, given that Sophie had laced her aubergine velvet corset dress with some gusto an hour or so back. They both wore the same outfits, a suggestive uniform that set the tone perfectly, both sophisticated and sexy as sin. The three freshly trained boutique staff were similarly attired and almost as excited as she was. She glanced up as Lucien appeared in the doorway.

"Got five minutes?" he asked. Even Kara had to admit he looked lethal, dressed in black from head to toe, the perfect canvas to set off his bronzed Viking looks. "Looking good, Mr. K," she grinned, following him towards the bar. And then she saw Dylan, and acknowledged that good as Lucien looked, he didn't have the same flip-flop effect on her heart as the beautiful American currently popping the cork on a bottle of vintage champagne.

Sophie was perched on a high stool at the bar, laughing at something Dylan had said. Lucien crossed to stand behind her, his fingers idly toying with the laces down the back of her corset.

"If you keep that up, the boutique customers will get more than they bargained for," she said dryly, wriggling her shoulders to stop him from inadvertently loosening her bodice.

"You can keep it on for now. But I get to take it off later," he murmured, for Sophie's ears only.

"Are we celebrating already?" Kara asked, accepting the glass that Dylan held out to her. His fingers brushed warm against hers. She noticed how his eyes were drawn to her mouth and lingered for a beat longer than could be considered polite, and knew that whatever was going on inside his head that very second would be deliciously filthy. A month spent in his bed had taught her that he was a man who loved sex voraciously, and when it came to him the feelings were mutual. She couldn't get enough. They screwed, and she just wanted him all over again, only harder. Rinse and repeat. He had a way of making her feel alive and beautiful, as if her every curve was his idea of perfection. He went straight to her head, and she found that she just wanted more, more, more.

"Okay. Doors open in fifteen, and we all need to be outside to meet and greet. The press are out in force from what I can see out there, so be ready to turn on the charm and smile for the cameras," Lucien said, his eyes on the screen of the outdoor surveillance monitor tucked away in the corner of the bar. No one noticed the frown that puckered Dylan's brow as he followed Lucien's gaze, sipping his champagne automatically.

"A toast," Lucien said turning back to them once they all had a glass in their hand. "To Gateway Ibiza, and all who screw in her."

Kara raised her glass to the others with a smile. She'd heard the toast several times, but it still amused her.

"To all who screw in her," she murmured, her eyes touching Dylan's again, knowing that he was thinking exactly the same as she was. *And to all those who've already screwed in her.*

Or was he? He looked more unsettled than he had a few moments ago, less relaxed. His laid-back Californian feathers definitely seemed ruffled to her eye, practised as it was at looking at him good and hard.

"So what's your plan tonight?" Kara asked him as Sophie and Lucien wandered away towards the office, his arm protectively around her waist. She leaned over the bar to afford Dylan a clear view down her Jessica Rabbit-style cleavage. "Because I can offer you a really special discount if you come by the boutique. What's your poison, Sailor?" she murmured, touching the folded back sleeve of his slate grey shirt. "Cuffs?" She circled her fingers firmly around his wrist, feeling the beat of his pulse beneath her thumb pad when she pressed down. "Nipple clamps?" She shimmied her shoulders to jiggle her breasts, gratified by the way his expression softened from tense to turned on. Whatever was on his mind, it was a thrill to know that she could make him forget about it. "Or maybe you'd like something a little kinkier..." she murmured, fucking him with her eyes. "Maybe you'd like to bend me over your knee and spank me with one of our leather riding crops. Because Dylan..." she whispered, pausing to lick her lips. "When this place closes tonight, I plan on being a very, *very* bad girl."

Outside ten minutes later, and the place was alive with queuing customers and the flash of cameras hungry for a shot of Lucien Knight, patron saint of the world of erotic clubs. They'd gone to great pains to create Hollywood red carpet-style glamour for the opening night, although the carpet was deep purple rather than scarlet. It was soon obscured by VIP guests milling around and posing for the cameras before entering the club, all keen to be portrayed as risque to enhance their images. Lucien and Sophie stood to the side giving interviews to the press, and he turned to beckon Dylan and Kara across for a photograph of the management team.

Kara nodded across the hordes in acknowledgement and placed her hand on Dylan's arm. "We're needed," she murmured, leaning close so as not to interrupt the conversation he was holding with a group of excited first night attendees. The scent of him filled her head, making her want to lick his neck. He turned to her with a smile, which slid from his face as his gaze moved to Lucien and Sophie and the waiting press photographer.

He excused himself from the conversation, his mind racing. He badly didn't want to let Lucien down tonight, this was the acid test. Equally, he didn't want his image splashed across tomorrow morning's local papers, or more worryingly, over the pages of entertainment industry magazines. The slim chance that someone back home would see the picture was enough to bathe his body in clammy foreboding. He followed Kara slowly because there was no other choice that he could see.

A few weeks here and already this place and these people felt dangerously like home. He didn't want it entangling with his former life. *Fuck*.

He met Lucien's eyes as he drew close, and saw the question in them. Was it written all over his face how much he didn't want to be photographed?

"So much charisma in one photograph," Kara said, linking her arm through Sophie's, her eyes on Dylan and Lucien. "Hope they don't break the camera lens."

Lucien reached into his pocket for his phone, flicked the screen on for a second and frowned.

"Sorry guys, minor emergency," he murmured to the photographers. "Dylan, the DJ's having some last minute hitches with the energy supply. Would you go and see what's going on? We open in five." Lucien moved between Sophie and Kara, an arm around each of their waists. "A thorn between two roses," he smiled graciously for their benefit, jerking his head imperceptibly at Dylan to disappear.

Moving away into the safety of the crowd, Dylan was well aware that the DJ would not be waiting for his help. He let his breath out on a long, slow huff. That had been close. Too close, and he now owed Lucien his thanks and some kind of explanation. He'd already been more economical with the truth than sat easily with his conscience. He really didn't want to lie to these people, but there was no way he was dragging them into his mess.

Chapter Eighteen

A couple of hours later, and Dylan was too busy and too fascinated to give any more thought to his problems. The club was full to capacity, the opening night guests were spending freely on cocktails and champagne, and the steady, sexy beat of the music provided a perfect backdrop to the scene unfolding in front of him.

He knew clubs like the back of his hand, but not this one.

He knew clubbers like the back of his hand, but not these people.

They had the same exterior gloss as conventional clubbers, more so, actually. They were exquisitely groomed and dressed to impress, albeit in flesh-revealing outfits and in some cases, lingerie. He'd ducked into the boutique earlier and found it full of interested customers, with Kara in her element as she helped someone choose between two different vibrators. He laughed softly as he moved back towards the bar, remembering back to the first time he'd met her, brandishing a vibrator at him like a gun. She sure was a woman of many facets. Unflinchingly honest, sexy beyond words, and sweet as spun sugar on the inside and out.

Around him, people drank and danced, warming up for the night ahead. There was a sense of expectation in the air, an alive, sexual pulse that throbbed through the entire place. He was finally experiencing the difference between this club and any other he'd managed. Here there was a sense of freedom and of daring, of anything being possible for those brave enough to grasp the opportunity.

Lucien appeared as he moved around the bar and checked in with the staff.

"Walk with me."

His low tone brooked no argument, not that Dylan would have shied away in any case. He needed to clear things up with Lucien, to show him that the trust he'd placed in him was not misdirected. Satisfied that all was well behind the bar, he caught up alongside his boss as he began to weave through the throng. Together they worked their way around the periphery of the club.

"What do you think?" Lucien asked. Dylan heard in the question confidence and pride but also a desire for reassurance. He knew how much this mattered to Lucien.

Dylan took a few seconds, drinking in the images around him. Dancers. Couples entwined around each other. Groups of revellers in the booths, a few celebrity faces among them. Their clothes would stay firmly on, but their status would be enhanced by gossip column inches and pictures the next day. Dylan knew that most of them were there at the behest of their PRs and advisors, targeted carefully by a comprehensive Gateway publicity campaign.

Champagne corks were flying. Nearby, a woman naked from the waist up ground slowly against the guy behind her, her eyes closed as his hands moved over her breasts.

A regular club with added erotic extras.

"I think it's fucking amazing," he said truthfully.

Lucien nodded, leading the way through to the spa area. Things had certainly kicked up a gear since Dylan had last been in there an hour back. Several people lounged naked in the jacuzzi, talking, flirting, and as he watched, one woman turned to another beside her and kissed her lingeringly, their bared breasts pressed together as their arms moved around each other. It wasn't so much exhibitionism as uninhibited freedom, a distinction Dylan hadn't fully appreciated until then. When a third woman joined them, he glanced away, back to Lucien's knowing eyes. It was a hard line to walk, being here in a professional capacity rather than as a pleasure seeker. He supposed it was like being on the set of a classy porn movie and having to keep your jeans on.

"It's natural to be turned on by it. It's the best fucking job in the world," Lucien said, interpreting Dylan's thoughts without difficulty. "It gets easier to detach in one way, but the day you stop wanting to strip off and fuck someone is the day to walk away. You need a healthy appreciation for sex to do this job justice."

A healthy appreciation for sex was one way to put it. A burning desire to hunt Kara down and screw her hard against the wall in the next five minutes was another.

Lucien headed up the nearby staircase at a jog, a man at ease in his environment. Dylan followed, knowing that if what he'd seen downstairs was any kind of yardstick, then upstairs was going to blister his eyeballs.

"This is how it'll be here, night in, night out. People come to drink and to fuck, simple as that. No drugs, no fighting, just fucking."

"As someone who has managed some rough clubs over the years, that is music to my ears, man," Dylan said, peering into one of the playrooms as they passed the open doorway. Seven or eight naked clubbers writhed on the oversized bed, a nest of nude bodies, their mouths feasting on each other. Painted lips sliding over rigid cocks. Tongues lapping between spread legs. Hips banging hips, mouths sucking nipples. It was a veritable sex carnival, the players utterly lost in the acts of giving and receiving pleasure.

"There's an absolution and purity to fucking that strips people back to their primal core," Lucien said, and his eyes moved from the playroom to Dylan. "Life is filled with double meanings and hidden secrets. There's no hiding here."

They moved along from room to room, scene after scene of

sex, from vanilla through to deepest darkest kink, the kind of stuff Dylan had barely even considered let alone taken part in. And he was no prude. But Lucien's words sat heavier on his mind than the scenes unfolding before him. No hiding.

Was he hiding? And what kind of a man did that make him?

"Lucien, I know I've given you no reason to trust me."

Dylan watched the man he'd come to think of as a friend lift one shoulder, the other leaning on the doorframe of a room set out for people who liked a little pain along with their pleasure. Cages. Shackles. Whips. And suddenly Kara was foremost in his mind once again, her promise of being a very bad girl suddenly more real as he watched a blonde gasp with pleasure as a riding crop left red welts across her exposed ass.

"Trust is a strange thing. Sometimes we give it even though it hasn't been earned, because something in our gut tells us to," Lucien said, as the man swung the crop down on the woman's cheeks again. "She's putting her trust him, even though she probably doesn't even know his name." He went on, "And I'm trusting you with my club and my friend, even though I'm well aware that I don't even know your name."

Dylan nodded. That didn't surprise him. Lucien was way too acute not to have looked into Dylan Day's background. He'd have done the same himself in the other man's shoes.

"And I don't need to know it," Lucien said, turning abruptly from the door and walking towards the stairs at the far end of the corridor. "But whatever trouble you're in obviously has you running scared. I've been that man, Dylan. It's tiring, isn't it?"

Dylan leaned his back against the wall at the top of the quiet stairwell.

"Fucking exhausting."

Lucien looked away for a few seconds and shook his head, then looked back again. "Can I help?"

Dylan huffed softly. "I appreciate that more than you'll ever know, man, but no. No one can." He pushed his hands through his hair. "And just so you know, my troubles are my own, and hand on heart, they will not and cannot follow me here. Your trust is not misplaced."

He stood with his hand outspread on his chest, feeling his heart beating too fast for comfort. He wouldn't lie, but the truth wouldn't come out either. It had no place here, and Lucien's opinion of him would inevitably change. Right now it meant a lot to count him as a friend.

They both turned at the sound of footsteps and found Kara coming up the staircase.

"Hey Sailor. I'm on break. Keep me company?"

Lucien placed his hand on Dylan's shoulder for the briefest of seconds, then left him to Kara's ministrations.

"What was that all about?" Kara asked, gazing after Lucien.

"Boy stuff."

Kara arched her eyebrows with a grin. "Boy stuff, huh? Dylan and Lucien, sitting in a tree..."

Dylan dropped his hands to Kara's waist. "The way you look in this outfit?" He ran his palms appreciatively over her velvet-clad hips and pulled her against him. "Not a chance."

Kara wound her arms around his neck. "I've got ten minutes," she murmured, kissing the golden hollow at the base of his neck and sliding her hand down over his crotch. "Take me somewhere private and find out what's underneath this dress?"

Dylan didn't need any further encouragement. He felt in his back pocket for his keys as he tugged her down the stairs. "In here." He flicked through the keys to the right one and slid it into the lock, not easy with Kara already wrapped around him, sliding her hands inside his shirt.

In the darkness, he reached for her.

"Tell me this isn't the broom cupboard," she whispered, her nimble fingers already unbuckling his belt.

"It's the broom cupboard." Dylan rucked Kara's dress up her thighs, running his hands over her stocking tops.

"You sure know how to show a girl a good time."

"You betcha," he muttered. "I wish I could see you. Stockings make me horny."

Kara freed his cock into her waiting hands. "I can tell."

"Fuck… English," he groaned. "You're pretty good at that."

"I know."

Dylan pulled Kara's lace knickers to the side and backed her against the wall. It was her turn to groan. "You're pretty good at that."

"I know," he said, exploring inside her. "I've been thinking about you all night." He lifted her and pinned her against the wall with his body. "Thinking about fucking you."

"So do me."

"Do me?" Dylan reached into his back pocket for a condom and sheathed himself. "You sound like a teenager," he murmured, thrusting his cock deep into her, making her cry out.

"It was your idea to screw in a cupboard," she panted, dragging his mouth onto hers.

"It was a good idea," he said, fucking her hard, loving the sounds she made and the way she wrapped her leg around his ass to clamp him close.

"The best," she said, her voice trembling when he reached down and fingered her slick clitoris. She was going to come, he knew it and she knew it, and he put his hand over her mouth to muffle her yells. He held her up with the weight of his body, his hips pumping hard as he let go of his control.

"The best," he repeated, lowering her slowly back down to her feet. He kissed her slowly, smoothing her dress back into place regretfully as she stroked his hair. "The best, English."

Chapter Nineteen

"I'm bushed." Kara fished around in her bag for the keys to the Mustang as she walked back to the car with Dylan at the end of the night.

He held out his hand. "Let me drive."

She handed them over willingly and flopped into the passenger seat.

"Remember to drive on the right."

"We drive on the right in the States," he said. "It's only you guys who do it the wrong way."

"The right way," she objected automatically, closing her eyes and enjoying the sensation of being taken care of.

Dylan threw his arm over the back of her seat and glanced over his shoulder as he reversed. "You have good taste in cars."

"Mmm. I seem to have a thing for all things American at the moment."

"You have a thing for me, English?" Delicious, sexy humour threaded its way through his drawl.

"Hmm," Kara said. "You. Mustangs." She yawned. "You."

"You said me already."

"Like New York," she muttered, half asleep. "So good I said you twice."

When she opened her eyes again, she was in Dylan's arms being carried along the pathway at the edge of the beach.

"I did not go to sleep," she said, nuzzling her face into his neck to get closer to the scent of him.

"Of course not," he said. Then added, deadpan, "But you

were snoring."

She opened her eyes wide. "I so was not."

"You've turned into that teenager again," he said, kissing her softly as they approached the boat. He set her on her feet and held her hand as she stepped aboard.

"Coffee?" she asked as he unlocked the door.

Dylan moved in close behind her in the small kitchen and kissed her shoulder.

"You sure you don't want to go straight to bed?"

"You've woken me up now. Let's have coffee first," she said, flicking the gas on beneath the kettle. He shrugged assent and turned on the radio, the station playing slow, chill-out tracks designed to lull the island's clubbers to sleep.

Dylan carried their mugs down into the living area a couple of minutes later and sat down on the lurid couch that ran around the edge. Kara dropped next to him, her head on his shoulder and her feet propped on his knees.

"So. First night done," she said, accepting her mug from Dylan.

He settled back, his own mug in his hand. "It sure had some highlights."

Kara touched her mug against his with a lazy smile. "To Gateway Ibiza, and all who screw in her broom cupboard."

They fell silent, both tired and still coming down from the high of the successful launch. Dylan looked out over the dark, star-studded skies. Dawn was still a couple of hours away.

I love this time of morning," he said quietly, his eyes on a lone fisherman in the distance loading nets into his vessel. "My brother Billy used to night fish."

Kara stilled, surprised by his words. It was the first time he'd volunteered any personal information.

"Are you close?"

"We were." Dylan drank deeply from his mug, letting the coffee scald his throat for a pain he could concentrate on. "He died a few of years back."

"Shit." Kara placed her mug down and sat up, her arm along

the cushion behind him. "I'm sorry, darlin'." She stroked the warm skin at the back of his neck, waiting to see if he wanted to say more. She hoped he would.

"It was a rough time." Dylan swallowed hard. "Still is. My mom struggles."

Kara blew out slowly, thankful that she was unable to comprehend the level of grief.

"Do you have any other brothers or sisters?"

Dylan's breath left his body in a long sigh. "One other brother. Justin." A different bleakness lined his face. "We're not so close."

There was obviously much that he wasn't saying, but she was delicate enough not to push him.

"I have twin brothers," she said instead. "They're seven years younger than me and drive me crazy most of the time."

Dylan laughed softly. "I bet their friends have crushes on you."

"What can I say?" she grinned. "I'm irresistible."

Dylan stroked her thigh. "You are."

Kara's stomach flipped at his serious reaction to her flippant remark.

"You are completely and utterly fucking irresistible," he said. "So how the hell are you still single?"

"Am I?" she said.

"You know what I mean, English," he chided.

Kara's grip tightened around her coffee mug. She knew what he meant.

"You really want to know?" she asked, not sure that she really wanted to tell him.

He nodded, his perceptive eyes searching.

"I was with the same guy for five years. He asked me to marry him and then forgot to turn up."

"No fucking way," Dylan said. He was genuinely astonished. Kara, jilted? He couldn't imagine anyone daring.

"Yes fucking way. Turned out he *forgot* quite a lot of things. Like to tell me about his other women, or the fact that one of them had threatened to gatecrash the wedding if he went through with it."

"He sounds like a piece of work."

Kara shook her head. "You don't know the half of it. He lied, and he lied, and he lied. I hate liars." She didn't look up to see Dylan's expression. Now that she'd started to talk the words were tumbling out, unchecked. "And the best of it is that you'd think I'd have been able to spot a liar, because my dad was the king of them all."

An unexpected lump rose in her throat. *Why the fuck was she telling him all of this?* But his hand was still warm and comforting on her leg. She wanted to get it out now. She wanted him to know all about her. To understand.

"He lied about pretty much everything, to all of us. To me, to my brothers, and to my mum. I haven't seen him since I was twelve years old."

Dylan sighed, and Kara looked up with a small smile. "So there you have it. I'm single because I'm the idiot who was stood up at the altar."

"You were definitely not the idiot in that story," Dylan said, drawing her against him and kissing her hair.

"It doesn't bother me any more. It did, but now it doesn't. It seems that you've cured me."

Dylan's mouth moved over her face, kissing her damp lashes.

"Promise me you'll never lie to me?" she said when he finally reached her lips.

"Kara…" he murmured, and then he kissed her until she had forgotten she'd even asked a question, let alone noticed that he hadn't answered.

The boat rocked in gentle motion to the slow beat of the music as Dylan's tongue slid between Kara's lips, exploring the sweetness of her mouth, trying to forget the things she'd said. Her father was a liar. Her ex was a liar. *He was a liar.*

Her fingers picked open the buttons of his shirt and smoothed it from his shoulders.

"You know, it's a crime to have that thing in here and not dance," she whispered, standing up, still holding his hand. He flicked his eyes to where she was looking, at the outlandish glitter ball slowly rotating above the lounge, and then shrugged with a half smile and stood up.

They smooched slowly, two late night lovers moving to lovers' music on a dance floor made just for them, arms wrapped around each other, their mouths grazing each other's shoulders. Dylan unpicked the laces of Kara's corset, making his fingers work patiently but so badly wanting her skin against his, her heat to warm him, her body to hold him.

Her dress slid off in his hands, leaving her beautiful in lacy lingerie and stockings. She was tired in his arms, pliant, yet still her nipples beaded against the lace and her hips undulated into his when he held her close. Her skin was silk against his, warm and vital, and the need to stay there in her arms blindsided him.

"The most perfect girl in the world," he said, his mouth against her ear, only half aware that the words had come out loud.

She pulled him closer until they pressed against each other from shoulder to hip, and a sigh of pleasure left her lips when he stroked her back. Dylan buried his face in her hair, loving her some, despising himself more. He understood her so much better after what she'd told him tonight, and he hated the knowledge that he was the next liar in her life.

Over at the villa, Lucien finally got to unfasten the laces on the back of a similar dress and make love to the woman he adored. He needed Sophie as he needed oxygen. She was the reason he could sleep at night and the reason he got up in the morning. He buried his cock deep inside her in the centre of their big bed, and he knew with complete certainty that he wanted to screw only this woman for the rest of his life. Married. He felt the passion in the idea growing, captivating him.

My Sophie. Soon to be my wife.

Dylan woke to the sounds of Kara moving around overhead. His watch told him that he'd slept in late: he could hear the whistle of the kettle and the sound of Kara singing along to the radio. Stumbling as he pulled on his jeans, he made his way up the ladder.

"Morning sleepyhead," she smiled, a vision in his shirt as she poured water into the coffee cups. "I made breakfast."

She held up a brown paper bag and he caught a waft of cinnamon. An image of her going to the bakery dressed in his shirt filled his head, pleasingly.

"You really should think about bringing a few things down here. Clothes... that kind of stuff..." he trailed off, aware of the significance of the suggestion.

She laughed, making the most of the moment.

"You asking me to move in with you, Sailor?"

He rolled his eyes, carrying their coffee up onto the roof terrace as Kara followed him with the pastries. They sat at the small rickety table, the sun already hot on their exposed skin. Kara dropped her sunglasses down over her eyes, messy-haired and looking deliciously like a woman who'd spent the night not sleeping a whole lot in a lover's bed. Which she had, of course. *His bed.* An unexpected wave of possessiveness swept over him from nowhere. He wanted to be the only man who got to spend the night with her.

She opened the bag and handed him a pastry.

"You're a fabulous cook," he said, biting into it.

"You did say *cook*?" she said, raising her eyebrows suggestively as she smoothed the bag out over her knees to serve as a plate. The double whammy of sugar and strong coffee seeped into their bloodstreams and worked its magic, revving them up for the new long day and night that lay ahead.

"I'll bring some clothes by later," she said, and, as simple as that, they agreed to spend the next couple of months together on the Love Tug.

"And about what I said last night..." she said conversationally, ripping the warm pastry apart with her fingers. " I meant every word of it, Dylan Day. Lie to me and I'll cut your cock off and pickle it."

Chapter Twenty

The club went from strength to strength over the following few weeks, as did Dylan and Kara's love-in on the Love Tug. Every day she fell a little deeper for the laidback American's charm, and he fell a little harder for her English sense of humour and disarming honesty. They worked hard, and they played hard, from sunny afternoons around the pool with Lucien, Sophie and Tilly to long steamy interludes that made the Love Tug rock despite the serene seas.

They found things they shared in common: a love of Thai food and horror movies.

They found things they were never going to agree on: the merits of reality TV and punk music.

But most of all they found solace in each other's arms, and peace in each other's body. Each new act of sex bonded them closer. Sometimes slow, intimate and intense, other times red hot sexy rip-your-shirt-off-and-fuck-me-right-now, but always consuming.

Dylan's skin turned a deeper shade of gold lying out on the deck with Kara, and he lowered his guard enough to feel insulated from the worries of his old life.

Settled. Happy, even.

It turned out to be the biggest mistake of his life.

Chapter Twenty-One

A stranger on a hired moped followed Kara's red Mustang along the coast road, his face obscured by a helmet.

He watched as she and Dylan parked the car and disappeared into the closed up club just after lunchtime.

He watched Kara leave again half an hour later and contemplated following her, catching up with her first instead. That would make for a *very* illuminating conversation. Tempting as it was, given the way her luscious ass had looked in those cut off denim shorts, he decided against it. He had more to gain from going inside.

He walked around the perimeter of the club, noting the dusty Estrella beer truck unloading, with professional interest. He slipped soundlessly into the unlocked cellar with the ease of a practised thief, waiting for a few minutes after the sound of the delivery truck's engine faded away before he unfurled himself from behind the crates. Helping himself to a bottle of beer, he knocked the lid off and drank deeply. A second beer followed the first, for Dutch courage. Now he was ready.

Upstairs in the office, Dylan worked on the staff rosters for the coming month, deep in concentration.

Downstairs behind the bar, Lucien flicked through the morning's mail, an espresso on the bar beside him. He'd left Sophie at home with Tilly for an afternoon of wedding planning with Kara, or more likely a wide-ranging chat over a glass of wine, if Kara had anything to do with it.

A sound behind him had him instantly on high alert, and he looked up a second before the man appeared through the door at the end of the bar.

"Who the fuck are you?" the stranger blurted, clearly not expecting his company.

"That's a fairly fucking audacious question, given the circumstances," Lucien said coolly, placing his cup down as he watched the smaller man with shrewd eyes. The guy's attire suggested that he was a holidaymaker, and a vain one at that. Cheap shorts, vest cut to show off his physique, a flashy identity bracelet and a thick chain around his wrist. Aggression emanated from him in waves, and only some vague familiarity in his face stopped Lucien from removing him by force from the premises without bothering to ask any more questions.

"Get your boss down here, man," the guy said. "And I'll have a Southern Comfort while I wait. In fact, make it a double."

Lucien made no move, considering the intruder's American accent. The stranger mistook his silence for trepidation, and reached arrogantly for a glass.

"No? I guess I'll just get my own then."

He had misread the situation. Big-time. His hand froze half way back down from the shelf as Lucien took a step towards him and said, his voice laden with menace,

"No you won't. Put *my* glass down and get the fuck out of *my* club." The stranger blanched and took several steps back and around the bar.

"You have precisely ten seconds before I post you home to your mama in a series of blood-stained envelopes," Lucien added, conversationally.

The guy slid the glass he'd snagged back onto the bar and swallowed hard. Then, both turned sharply at the sound of footsteps jogging down the stairs. A couple of seconds later, Dylan emerged through the staff doorway.

"Lucien, do you know whether…" Dylan's words died in his mouth as he caught sight of the visitor.

Lucien watched Dylan's expression go from easy to stricken, and the pieces tumbled into place. The man was a stranger to Lucien, but not to Dylan. Now he knew why he'd had the sense of recognising something in his face.

"Hey big bro," the guy said, oily now that he felt he had the upper hand again. "Long time no see."

"Justin." Dylan could not have loaded the word with more despondency if he'd tried. He threw the paperwork in his hand down on a nearby table. "What the fuck are you doing here?"

His heart thumped uncomfortably behind his ribs. How long had Justin been here? What had he said to Lucien?

"That's no way to welcome your little brother, is it?" Justin said, the same sly grin on his face that always irritated the hell out of him.

"How did you find me?" Dylan said flatly. He hated the fact that Lucien had to hear this.

Justin practically sneered. "Because you couldn't help sucking up to mom, even from thousands of miles away." It figured that their mother would have trusted Justin around her computer. She always wanted to think the best of him. "*Hey mom, I remembered Billy's birthday,*" Justin said, affecting a mocking, whiney voice.

"*Hey Matthew, you've always been a good boy, Justin's always been the bad boy. Stay in Ibiza and enjoy yourself while he rots,*" Justin went on, an awful impersonation of their mother that hit the mark anyway. "Just like you let Billy rot." Those weren't their mother's words, they were pure Justin.

Dylan's heart constricted with pain at the low jibe. He looked at his brother for several long, silent seconds, searching for something worth loving and coming up with nothing. As kids they'd shared little in common, as men even less. There was an underhand slyness to his kid brother that had made Dylan's skin crawl his whole life.

"Go home, Justin. You have no place here."

"And yet it seems you do, Matty." Justin gestured around the club, the bracelets on his wrist clashing against each other in the quiet room. Dylan flinched at the sound of Billy's nickname for him, his eyes sheering away from Lucien's unreadable ones across the room.

"Maybe I see what you've got going here and I want in. I saw that hot piece of ass you were with earlier." Justin cut an hourglass shape in the air with his hands. "Maybe I want in on *that*, too."

It was debatable who reached him first. Within a second he was surrounded, Dylan on one side, Lucien on the other, fury white hot on both faces. Like prey caught between two prowling lions, Justin's eyes darted for an escape route, knowing there wasn't one.

"Okay, okay," he said nervously, holding his hands up. His bravado had dissolved once again. "At ease, boys."

Neither Lucien nor Dylan moved a muscle.

"For mom's sake, I'm going to let you walk out of this place alive," Dylan said, his voice low and steady.

"And for *Matthew's* sake, I'm going to give you until night fall to leave the island before I send out for those envelopes," Lucien said in his ear, his fist itching to smack into their intruder's jaw. Hearing his emphasis on the name, Dylan couldn't meet Lucien's eye.

"And I came all this way just to deliver your mail," Justin said, rallying slightly, drawing a beige, official-looking envelope out of his back pocket. Dylan took it from him, not even glancing at it.

"Get out," he said heavily, feeling the fragile new life he'd built for himself unravelling thread by slow thread.

He watched his brother leave with Lucien close on his heels. He sank down onto the nearest chair, shoving the envelope addressed to Matthew McKenzie into his back pocket and dropping his head into his hands.

Outside, Lucien pinned Justin up against the wall with a hard shove. Edgy and rigid with fury, he towered over the other man in both stature and power. In that moment, he wasn't Lucien Knight, lover and father. He was Lucien Knight, loyal friend, the man you'd want in your corner when the chips were down. The man you really didn't want to be on the wrong side of.

"You speak to no one, or I will know. You go straight to the airport, or I will know. You board a plane, or I will know. Set foot on Ibiza again, and I will know." He leaned his arm against Justin's wind pipe, his face inches from the other man's. "Have I made myself clear, or do you need me to fucking spell it out?"

The shifty fear in Justin's eyes answered for him. He was on his way. He was a low life of no substance or worth, and he thought too much of his charmless face to risk its rearrangement by such a formidable foe.

Lucien watched the younger man walk away, certain that he would never lay eyes on him again.

Justin made his way back to the airport, his pride stinging and his throat sore, but satisfied that he'd thrown a grenade into his brother's life in the form of a screwed up, beige envelope.

Chapter Twenty-Two

Lucien walked back into the club, passed by Dylan's table, and strode straight to the bar. Two glasses and a bottle of vodka in his hands, he returned and pulled up a chair at the table.

"Do you mind if I stick to Dylan?" His tone was neutral. "I'm kind of used to it." He poured two good measures and pushed one across the table.

Dylan scrubbed his palms into his eye sockets. "I'm sorry, man." He didn't have any words to explain the weight his brother's unexpected appearance had dropped back onto his shoulders. His hard won peace had dissolved around him like ice on a hot day, showing up his life on Ibiza for the cheap illusion of smoke and mirrors it was.

There was a long silence. They both drank a measure, not meeting eyes.

"So. You're nothing like your brother," Lucien said, eventually.

Dylan swallowed the remaining contents of his glass in one mouthful.

"That's just about the best thing anyone's ever said to me."

Lucien refilled Dylan's glass.

"There were three of us. Billy. Me. Justin." Dylan didn't raise his eyes from the bottom of his glass. "Billy was the best of all of us. Now there's just me. And *him*."

"What happened?" Lucien watched Dylan's face as he searched for the right words, and he recognised the expressions that twisted his features. Grief, and guilt. He recognised them because he'd shouldered the same emotions for too many years himself over someone he'd loved too.

"Billy… he was my big brother, and… my best friend. Sunshine followed him into every room, you know?"

Lucien didn't know. Not when it came to family, anyhow, but for the first time he was learning it now about a friend. Dylan had brought a new aspect to his life that he hadn't even known had been missing. Brotherhood.

"He got himself into trouble… gambling… debts he couldn't make… I missed the signs. Too busy on my way up to notice, and he was too proud to come to me." Dylan swirled the vodka in his glass, and Lucien sat still, in silent solidarity opposite him.

"They found him hung by his own belt out in the woods behind his house. Open and closed case." Dylan shrugged, his face etched with disgust.

"Was it?"

"Hell, no. Billy was no coward, and no matter how much shit he was in he'd never have broken our mother's heart that way, on purpose."

Lucien's affinity with the man opposite increased with his every word. Both of their lives had been overshadowed by loss and consumed by guilt. The difference between them was that Lucien had worked his way out the other side, thanks to Sophie. Dylan was still living in his own version of hell, and his brother's appearance had just turned up the heat to unbearable levels. To Lucien's eyes, he looked very much as he had the first time they'd met. Beat.

"Justin has been spoiled his whole life. He grew up with a sense of entitlement, for no good reason. He was always going to get himself in trouble, and I was always going to be the one who had to bail him out. I think he gambled too just to prove he could succeed where Billy failed, to be the big man. Except he wasn't. He got in way over his head, debt on debt, and then he came to me with his hands out. *They're going to kill me, they're going to take mom's house.*" Unconsciously, Dylan adopted his brother's drawling tone, his expression miserably disgusted. He shook his head, his eyes still downcast. "So I bailed him." He shrugged. "It took my club and my home, but I did it, because I couldn't fail a brother again."

"And then you came here?"

Dylan nodded. "I didn't plan on lying." He knocked back the vodka. "I just wanted to be someone else for a while. To get away. Just…" He tailed off.

Lucien sighed heavily. He could understand that.

"Seems to me that you've pulled it off pretty well up to now," he observed.

"I was a fool to think I could make it work." Dylan's tone was savage, castigating himself.

"Way I see it, nothing has changed."

Dylan's laugh held no trace of humour. "I don't think Kara is going to see it that way. She deserves so much better than another liar in her life."

"She told you, huh?"

Dylan nodded. "And trust me, I could not feel like a bigger shit than I do right now."

"Look," Lucien sighed. "I can't tell you what to do, and I won't lie to Kara and Sophie for you. But find your own way to tell her over the coming weeks. I won't push you. And in any case, I don't think that brother of yours is likely to come back any time soon."

Dylan nodded slowly. He recognised the wisdom of Lucien's words, and appreciated the trust he'd bestowed by allowing him to dictate the pace. His idyll had to end, but he could choose how and when. It was a bittersweet privilege.

"Don't underestimate Kara," Lucien said, leaning back on his chair. "She might just surprise you."

"She already does. Every single day."

Lucien nodded, cradling his glass in his hands. He knew a woman like that too, and he recognised in Dylan the signs of a man falling hard.

"About the wedding…"

Dylan looked up, his troubled expression clearing a little at the change of subject.

"We're keeping it low key," Lucien said. "Just a handful of people, and I... I kind of wondered if you'd be my best man."

Dylan was unaccustomed to hearing Lucien sound anything but ultra confident, making the trace of nerves behind his question all the more noticeable.

"I'd love to, man," he said, feeling the tension leave his body as he reached out and shook Lucien's hand, clasping it with both of his own. "I'd really love to."

The bond of friendship between the two men deepened as Dylan added more vodka to their glasses. Maybe there was hope, after all. Lucien would have been within his rights to ask him to leave, but he'd chosen instead to stand beside him, shoulder to shoulder.

"Thank you," Dylan said. "Your faith in me means a lot."

Lucien lifted a nonchalant shoulder. "Just don't expect me to hug," he said, pushing his chair back as he stood. "I like you, but this isn't Brokeback Mountain."

As Lucien walked away, Dylan couldn't repress an inner smile, a feeling of warmth, despite the disagreeable events of the evening, as he gazed into his shot glass. He hadn't only found a remarkable woman in Ibiza. He'd made a true friend.

At the villa, Kara and Sophie sat on the terrace beneath the shade of an umbrella, little needed now the evening had drawn in, an open bottle of chilled white wine on the table in front of them.

"Here in Ibiza? In a few weeks time?" Kara repeated Sophie's words. "I was looking forward to a trip to the land of sexy Vikings."

"Sorry. Blame my Viking. He wants to get married here."

Kara shrugged with exaggerated resignation. "I'm probably not in the market for a Viking anyway," she admitted.

"You've changed your tune," Sophie grinned, topping up their wine glasses. "I take it that the divine Mr. Day is the reason for your change of heart?"

"God, Soph," Kara said, feeling the flush of pleasure on her cheeks at the mention of him. "He really is divine. He's like… I don't even know how to put it. He melts me." Kara ignored Sophie's knowing smile. "I mean it, I've never met anyone like him before. It's like… he really gets me."

"And does he?" Sophie said, raising her eyebrows questioningly. " Does he *really* get you?"

"Holy fuck. Yes. God, yes!" Kara laughed. "Does he ever."

"Good. You deserve someone to make you feel like that," Sophie said. "God knows, you've kissed your share of frogs."

"You really think he might be my prince?"

"Any man who can make you blush like that gets my vote. I like him a lot Kara. I really do."

Kara lay back and closed her eyes, a serene smile on her face.

Maybe it *was* time for her luck to change. Dylan Day was the first man she'd ever met who seemed to genuinely want her for who she was, without any hidden agendas, without any skeletons in his cupboards, without any secret girlfriends waiting to jump out on her if she let herself get in too deep.

Maybe. Maybe it would be okay.

Kara really wanted it to be okay.

She realised that she believed it could be.

It would be. Really.

Chapter Twenty-Three

"What shall we do with our night off, Sailor?" Kara twirled Dylan's hair around her fingers, massaging his scalp as they lay baking on the deck of the Love Tug in the late afternoon sun.

Once a week, Sophie and Lucien gave them a precious night off together, and they did the same in return. Tonight was Kara and Dylan's turn to play hooky, and she wanted to kick back and make the best of every moment. With each day that slid by beneath the warmth of the Ibizan sun, she became more aware of how little time they had until the end of summer. And she resolutely wasn't thinking beyond that.

"Shall we take this little boat and sail off around the island?" she said.

Dylan rolled onto his side, his warm hand on her ribs as he looked down at her.

"Do you know how to sail this thing? Because lovely as it sounds, I don't have the first idea."

"Well that's that plan scuppered," Kara said. "Any more ideas?"

Dylan slid his hand down over her stomach, tracing his fingers along the edge of the triangle of her lime green bikini. "How 'bout I help you get out of this and take you downstairs, show you who's boss?"

Kara laughed. "Do you have handcuffs? Every good boss needs handcuffs."

"No. You want me to get some?"

"I already have some, and I might just have to fetch them and show *you* who's boss," she grinned, catching his wrists and encircling them with her hands. He let her hold him down for a few seconds, his eyes lazily turned on. "I might bring my whip too," she murmured, her chest against his as she slid her knee over his shorts-clad crotch.

"Will you wear black leather?" he asked, lifting his head to catch her kiss, letting his tongue flicker into her mouth.

"No." An amused glint lit her eyes. "You will."

He laughed, rolling her over and pinioning her beneath him with ease.

"You crossed the line, English." He restrained her wrists beside her head, his body deliciously heavy on hers. "You wear the leather, and I'll take it off you." He dipped his head and kissed her again, slow and easy this time, that world-class mouth of his stealing any argument that might have been in her. There were no two ways about it. She was wildly turned on by the idea of wearing leather for him and letting him take it off her.

"Soon then," she said, when he let her come up for air. "But not today." She stroked his back when he released her hands, enjoying his sun-warmed skin. "Take me somewhere new today. Take me on an adventure." She ran her hands over his ass, and he rocked his hips into hers.

"You know that wherever we go, the plan involves fucking, yes?" he said, kissing his way along her jaw. It was an entirely unnecessary question.

"In the Mustang," she whispered, grazing his earlobe with her teeth. "I want you to fuck me on the back seat."

He lifted his head, and that lazy turned on look in his eyes had notched up to crazy turned on.

"Say that again." The desire in his murmured voice turned her body inside out with lust. "Tell me again how you want me to fuck you."

Kara's smile took over her whole face as she wrapped her leg around his thighs tighter to bring his cock harder against her.

"Fuck me, Dylan Day. Drive me somewhere quiet and make

me come all over the back seat of the Mustang." She dragged her nails down his back. "I want you to strip me naked and bend me over the bonnet."

Dylan ground against her, making her lips part on a sigh of pleasure.

"Where I come from, it's a hood."

"Call it whatever you like, darlin'. Just bend me over it and screw me with your big, hard cock."

"You have a filthy mouth, English…" Dylan reached between their bodies and pushed her bikini top up over her breast so that he could roll her already rock-hard nipple between his thumb and fingers. "Tell me some more."

Kara opened her mouth, and he dropped his face to hers, all the heat from their conversation spilling into their hard, hungry kiss. She moaned, writhing beneath him, not caring if anyone could see them because her head only had room for him in it. "Dylan…" she breathed his name, her eyes closed. "Plan B. Let's not go anywhere. Take me downstairs." She bit gently on his lip. "Take me to bed."

He groaned into her mouth. "Much as I'd love to," - his hand covered her breast, warm and massaging - "I can't get the idea of the Mustang out of my head now."

Kara lifted her hips, cradling his erection between her legs. "I'm too far down the line, Sailor," she pleaded. "Don't make me wait."

He smiled, rocking himself against her. "It'll be worth it, I promise," he whispered, holding her face. "Next time you come you'll be sitting up on that folded down roof with my head between your legs."

Kara moaned against him, and he slid a finger into her mouth. "Can you see it, baby?"

She swirled her tongue around his finger, her eyes closed. She could see it, hell, she could feel it, but the fantasy just wasn't enough. He was driving her slowly out of her mind.

He stroked her hair back from her forehead with his other

hand, moving his hips into hers again.

"I'm gonna open you, and look at you, and put my mouth on you." He slid his finger in and then back out of her mouth again, running the tip over her damp lips before sliding it back inside. "I love the taste of you," he said against her ear. "Sweet as honey."

She was so close, moaning on every laboured breath, and he just wouldn't give her enough. "Please…"

"Beautiful girl," he said, and when she opened her eyes, his were serious and so full of raw emotion that he took her breath away.

"Get the keys, Sailor. We're going out right now."

In the car ten minutes later, Kara's body still burned hot for him beneath the cut-offs and vest top she'd thrown on over her bikini. He drove the Mustang with the same laid-back confidence he did everything else in his life, and as she watched his tanned hands on the wheel, she was already imagining them on her body instead.

She frowned when he turned down a lane and eased the Mustang into a parking space amongst a few other cars.

"I was hoping for somewhere more private," she said, taken aback, glancing around at the smattering of shops and restaurants.

"You're going to be hungry by the time I've finished with you. Let's get dinner to take out."

Dylan swung her door open for her, holding his hand out, and she grinned despite herself. "You know me too well."

"I sure know you well enough to know how cranky you get when you're hungry."

"Not as cranky as I'm going to get if you don't give me my orgasm soon."

"I have it right here," he said, running his finger across his mouth, catching her around the waist with his other arm. "It's on the tip of my tongue." He bent his head and kissed her, brief yet off the scale sexy. "Can you taste it?"

She nodded, barely. She could. He tasted of sex and promises as yet unmet.

He took her hand and steered her into the nearest store, picking up a basket as they went in.

There was something endearingly domestic about shopping with him for their post-orgasmic supper, and it heightened Kara's anticipation even more. He ran his hand down her back as she placed water into the basket, and she kissed his cheek when he leaned down for potato chips from a rack near the till. She chucked in a few beers next to the warm cheese- and ham-laden pastries he'd added, then a punnet of fresh strawberries too. Dylan chose marshmallows and a block of chocolate.

"For you. You're gonna need sugar for energy," he said, dropping the last couple of things in and smiling at the woman behind the counter as he set the basket down.

"Big talk," Kara murmured, adding a half bottle of brandy to the pile of provisions and watching him chat idly with the cashier as she rang their food through, packing it for him even though she hadn't packed for the customers ahead of them in the queue. He had a way about him that made people do things they wouldn't normally do. Women, anyway. He did it to her, to pretty much any other woman who crossed his path, and she was pretty sure he didn't even know he was doing it.

Come to think about it, it wasn't just women that Dylan Day charmed. Men and babies too, if Lucien and Tilly were any kind of yardstick. Lucien seemed more relaxed in Dylan's company than she'd ever seen him with another guy before, and Tilly had fallen for him on sight. He seemed to sprinkle his magic wherever he went, and Kara just wanted to stay close and mesmerised.

Plus she wanted that damn orgasm from him a hell of lot more than she wanted chocolate or strawberries or beer. She wanted it more than she wanted pretty much anything else, and then she knew full well that as soon as she'd had it she'd want another. Greedy as she might be, she wasn't planning on being selfish: she also intended to give Dylan Day some unforgettable memories of his own in return. That prospect in itself was seriously sexy.

The sun was starting to set as Dylan killed the engine on the Mustang, this time somewhere without any other cars in sight.

"This better?" He turned to Kara, who was looking out over the beautiful scene laid before her. They'd wound their way through a pine forest to a tiny, deserted beach. Dylan had parked the car on the fringes of the sand, and right in front of them the huge sun tracked low in the sky, casting long, peachy bands of shadow across the sea towards them.

"Better than that. It's perfect."

"I thought you'd like it." There was the tiniest suggestion of smugness in his voice.

Kara slanted her eyes at him, her eyebrows raised.

"You think you know me pretty well, huh?"

"I'm enjoying getting to know you better every day, English," Dylan said softly. With a slight change of tone, he added, "So, shall we walk for a while?"

"Or I could just climb into the back?" Kara was finding it hard to think about anything else right now.

"You could. There's something I want to do first though." He got out, coming around to open her door.

Kara gave in gracefully, swinging herself out of the car. "This better be good."

Dylan took her hand and led her towards the trees. "We need to gather firewood."

"Firewood?"

He nodded. "I'm gonna build us a campfire."

"Are we playing Scouts and stuff?" Kara said. "'Cause I have to tell you here and now, I was thrown out of the Girl Guides."

Dylan laughed, bending to gather sticks. "Why does that not surprise me?"

"Fraternising with the Scouts was frowned on, apparently."

Dylan whistled low. "You've got me almost wishing I'd joined the Scouts, back then."

"So why didn't you?"

He sighed, and Kara felt his melancholy despite the fact that he wasn't looking her way. "I guess we just weren't a Scouting kind of family."

She grinned when he turned towards her, anxious to restore his good humour.

"Thank God for that. You don't learn to kiss the way you do by being a good boy."

She stood on tiptoe to meet his mouth, his arms full of wood.

"Time to go back to the car yet?" she murmured when he let her up for air a few minutes later.

He placed the logs in her arms. "Soon. Go dump this on the beach. I'll be there in a sec."

Kara frowned, resigned. "You're not expecting me to sing Kum Ba Yah or anything, are you?"

"Sing what? No." He dropped his voice. "I'm expecting you to let me make you come by firelight."

She was suddenly hot all over and completely on board with the fire idea. The Mustang plan had been a great one, but sex by firelight was compelling enough for her to set it aside, for the moment at least.

"Okay. So, go gather wood, Sailor. Quickly."

Chapter Twenty-Four

When Dylan strolled out of the treeline five minutes later, it was all he could do not to drop all the wood he'd gathered.

Kara was naked. Stark naked, standing waiting for him with her hands on her hips, her hair falling in waves around her shoulders. The setting sun dappled her skin, turning her ethereal.

He walked closer, bending to lower the wood onto the sand.

"I always had a thing for mermaids," he said, reaching for the hem of his T-shirt and dragging it off over his head. "So very lovely," he murmured appreciatively, walking around her. "I used to wonder how they had sex." He ran his hand around her waist and pulled her back against his body, nestling himself against the softness of her backside, enjoying her soft intake of breath.

"Everyone knows our tails turn into legs on shore," she said, leaning her head back onto his shoulder.

Dylan moved one hand up to cover Kara's breast, and slid his other hand down to run the tip of his finger slowly into the crevice between her legs.

"You're definitely all woman right now," he said. Her nipple strained hard in his fingers as she stepped her feet wider apart on the sand to let him touch her more intimately.

"Make a really thorough check," she whispered, arching an arm up around his neck, her nails raking the skin at his nape.

Dylan squeezed her breast, kneading her flesh in his hand. "All in order here," he whispered. "Beautiful. Warm. Soft." He punctuated each observation with a rock of his hips.

"And here?" she said, covering his hand between her legs with her own.

Dylan groaned against her ear. "I think I need to investigate a little more."

He cupped her in his hand, enjoying the warmth of her palm holding him against her. She closed her eyes, and he watched her face in the dwindling twilight. *How could she look so fragile and yet so powerful at the same time?*

She trusted him. She told him so with her body, and he found himself needing to swallow hard as his fingers moved inside her folds. She moved him in a way no woman ever had before. Everything about her was honest, and each day was better because she was in it.

He kissed the corner of her mouth when she pulled her bottom lip between her teeth, waiting for him to touch her where she needed to be touched. She looked caught somewhere between pain and pleasure, surrendered, womanly.

He ran his free hand up her body and laid his forearm along the curve of her neck, his hand massaging the back of her skull. He kissed her because his mouth needed hers, deep, wide open kisses, as close as he could get. His tongue stroked inside her mouth as he spread her wide and exposed her clitoris, both of their hands on her.

Her fingers slid between his and he was suddenly hyper-aware of every sensation.

Her body was so ready for him. *Slick.*

Her head moved against his shoulder. *Restless.*

Her back was warm against his chest. *Pressed.*

Her hips undulated into his erection, massaging him. *Hard.*

She was right on the edge of her orgasm. *Shimmering.*

He built her up. *Steady.*

And then, at the very second he knew she couldn't take any more preamble, he pulled her hard against him and fingered her clitoris fully, giving her everything he had in an erotic onslaught. His mouth. His hands. His thrusts. His tongue. His moans.

She reacted instantaneously, her body shaking and juddering

as her orgasm hit her hard. *Jesus, she was beautiful. Abandoned. Totally fucking breath-taking.*

"Well?" Her voice shook when her eyes flickered open some seconds later, heavy-lidded with satisfaction. "Woman, or mermaid?"

He dropped his jeans on the sand and swung her up in his arms, walking out towards the sea.

"There's only one way to know for certain."

"You build a good fire for a boy who never took his Scouting oath."

Kara sat on the sand with her arms wrapped around her knees as Dylan added a couple of logs to the fire he'd built after their swim. Skinny dipping with a drop dead sexy man by silver moonlight was a memory she'd filed away in the 'keep forever' file, and sitting beside him in the firelight was another tableau she never wanted to forget.

Bare-chested and tousle-haired, he looked as if he'd been cast from gold. Solid, gleaming gold.

She sipped brandy straight from the bottle, letting the warmth of the alcohol burn slowly inside her mouth. Every bone in her body felt heavy, totally relaxed. Heart-stopping sex, a lazy swim, and the perfect makeshift dinner can do that to a girl.

She smiled as she watched Dylan spear a marshmallow on a stick he'd whittled into a skewer.

"You really are the all American boy," she smiled softly, watching him toast the candy over the flames.

He glanced up. "You think so?"

She nodded. "Hair, teeth and toasted marshmallows. Case closed."

"I see." He held out the stick, the golden-toasted marshmallow on the end of it.

"Is it going to burn me?"

"Not if you're cautious." He lifted his eyebrows. "Do you even know what the word means?"

Kara rolled her eyes. "I can be cautious. I just don't feel like I need to be where you're concerned."

She took the stick and lifted the marshmallow to her nose, taking in the sweet, burnt sugar smell. It reminded her of candyfloss, bought and greedily consumed on chilly evenings at the bonfire night funfair back home as a kid. But she wasn't cold tonight. She was warm inside and out from the fire Dylan had built on the sand, and in her heart.

Dylan heard Kara's words, felt her trust, and wanted more than anything for them to be true. He wanted to be the man she made him feel like he was, rather than the guy who'd let his brother die and lost everything he owned trying to save the other one.

Thoughts of Justin ran like a thief through his head, stealing his happiness away, leaving him empty and imprisoned by the awareness that he needed to tell Kara the truth.

And he would. He didn't know when, but he would. He'd honestly tried to a couple of times already, but each time the words got stuck behind his selfish need to stay on the pedestal where she'd put him. The view from up there was so good. Life with Kara was blue skies, mile wide smiles and smoking hot sex. The skies would no doubt still be blue after she knew, and he could survive without sex if he had to, but the idea of wiping that beautiful smile from her face nearly broke him.

Watching her now as she tried to exercise caution with the hot marshmallow, he knocked back a mouthful of brandy and tortured himself, wondering how she'd react. *Would she hate him? Would she be furious?* God, please let her be furious rather than cry, because he'd rather cut out his own tongue than make Kara cry.

He kidded himself that he wasn't like the other liars in her life. He was a liar by circumstance rather than choice, he wasn't hiding truths from her for his own benefit. *Or was he?* She didn't even know his name, for God's sake. She couldn't Google him, because she didn't know his name. She couldn't read all of the salacious scandal about his family, because she didn't know his name.

And the problem was that with every passing day, he wanted to stay Dylan Day more and more.

Kara held out the empty stick towards him.

"See? Cautious. And delicious." She licked her lips. "Do me another?"

Dylan pushed the stick into a second soft, white marshmallow, trying to shake off the blues and enjoy the moment. The firelight warmed Kara's skin tone to toffee and danced roses in her cheeks. She looked like the best cheerleader in the world.

He let himself imagine her for a couple of moments, all short skirt and pompoms, spelling out his name with that huge smile of hers on her face. 'Gimme a D...D.Y.L.A.N. D.A.Y!'

And there it was again. The big lie that sat between them. And he wanted more than anything for her to know the truth.

"What's on your mind, Sailor?"

He looked up from turning the stick close to the embers. She was way too in tune with his emotions. Could she see the mess inside his head? The darkness?

He sighed heavily. *Was this the right moment?*

"Here." He held out the stick. "It's ready."

Chapter Twenty-Five

Kara sensed Dylan's mood shift from carefree to pensive, despite the fact that he was clearly trying to cover it up. It wasn't the first time she'd sensed his withdrawal, and it confused the hell out of her. She wanted in... into his head, and into his body. And not just sometimes. All of the time.

Planting the used marshmallow stick in the sand, she scooted over and swung her leg over his jean-clad hips. Pleasure returned slowly to his face as she straddled his lap, wrapping her legs around his back and her arms around his shoulders.

"I'm treating you to the full-on, all-body Brookes special here," she said, loving the way his arms moved to hold her close even as the heavy sigh left his body. "This hug has been known to end wars."

An appreciative sound rumbled in Dylan's chest. "I can well believe that." He twisted her still damp hair in his fingers. "It's almost perfect."

Kara pulled her head back. "Almost?"

Dylan peeled off her vest top. They'd both pulled minimal clothing on after their swim.

"You're wearing stuff. You need to be naked to achieve war-ending status."

"Nice line, Sailor."

Kara climbed out of Dylan's lap and shimmied out of her cut-offs, dropping her vest top on the sand beside them. Back in position a couple of seconds later, she wrapped herself around Dylan for a second time.

"And now?" she asked.

"Fucking perfection," he said, scooping her close to sit on his erection, his crotch hot and hard between her spread legs.

"Am I?"

"Stop fishing, English."

"I just wanted to make you forget whatever it is that creeps up on you sometimes and steals your smile."

Dylan's hands roved over her back and ass, following her curves as if he were committing them to memory. He let his forehead rest on her shoulder for a few seconds, and Kara stroked the back of his head. His body language told her two things. He needed to talk, and he needed to fuck.

"So, tell me."

Dylan lifted his head, and the bleak expression in his eyes scared her hard. She wrapped her arms around him, her mouth close to his ear.

"Nothing you can tell me will make me run, Dylan."

He shook his head lightly and kissed her shoulder. "You don't know that, English."

She straightened in his lap, took his hands, and placed them over her breasts.

"You're right. I don't know that." Her nipples hardened as he circled them with his thumbs. "But I don't trust easily Dylan, and everything in me knows that I can trust you."

"You show me with the way you listen to me." She ran her hands down his arms, down the hard, lithe muscles from his shoulders to his elbows, grasping them to move herself even closer over the heat of his crotch.

"You show me with the way you touch me," she breathed, closing her eyes for a second as he measured the weight of her breasts in his hands, his eyes on her curves. She moaned a little when he dipped his head to close his mouth over one nipple and then the other, almost reverential.

"And you show me with the way you fuck me," she said, a catch in her breath when he moved his hand down between their bodies.

"I trust you, Dylan Day. Her mouth was just a breath from his. "Simple as."

Kara tilted her mouth over his and kissed him. Brandy, sugar, and Dylan Day, just about the most erotic flavour she'd ever tasted. The heat inside his mouth made her moan, his tongue slow and searching.

His kiss gave him an unfair advantage. If her hugs could stop wars, then Dylan's kiss was his secret weapon. His fingers stroked between her legs as he deepened their kiss, as natural as breathing and bone-deep sexy.

"Touching you makes me forget the bad stuff," he murmured, sliding two fingers inside her to the knuckle. Kara gasped, opening her eyes wide, breathless.

"So touch me some more." Suddenly this was an urgent priority, whatever the bad stuff was.

Dylan smiled against her lips, his other arm around her waist holding her close. Kara's mouth opened on a groan when his thumb covered her clitoris.

"Like this?" he said, massaging. He wasn't asking because he was unsure. He knew exactly what he was doing.

"Like that," she squirmed on his hand and tightened her legs around him as he thrust inside her.

He kissed her again and again, his tongue and his thumb moving in rhythm. She opened her eyes and looked into his, dark green glitter and more emotions than she knew what to do with.

"Let go, English," he said, screwing his fingers deep inside her, his thumb faster on her clitoris. "Let go."

And she did, and it made her yell his name and clutch him close until they were skin to skin. The weight of his arm around her waist held her down on his thrusting hand, making her come harder, longer, louder, and he kissed her right through it until she fell against his chest, spent.

Dylan smoothed her hair back from her face when she lifted her head again a few minutes later. She swam back slowly into the moment, recalling the unfinished conversation.

"Feel like talking, Sailor?" she said softly, needing him to let her in.

His eyes moved from her face and settled on the distant lights of a boat out at sea.

"I guess so."

His words sounded resigned, and twilight closed in across his expression. She wasn't even sure why she was pushing him, except for the need to be able to help him, to know what put those shadows beneath his beautiful eyes so she could chase them right away again.

He'd shared barely anything with her aside from the fact that his brother had passed away. Was he still grieving? She couldn't begin to fathom the magnitude of a loss like that.

She laid her hands on his shoulders, massaging.

"Is it your brother?" She prompted him gently, offering him a hook to make the conversation easier to start. His eyes flicked to hers, unreadable.

"Billy."

One small word, and a whole world of longing. Kara's heart broke a little watching Dylan search for the words to tell her whatever he needed her to know.

"He died because of me."

Shit. Her heart didn't just break a little, it cracked wide open.

"What happened?" She wasn't massaging his shoulders any longer, she was gripping onto them. Onto him.

"I let him down. Didn't see he was in trouble. I was going up, and he was going right down, and I never stood still long enough to notice." Dylan shook his head, his eyes far away, remembering. "I'd got everything I thought I ever wanted. Flashy club. Fancy home. Fast cars." He made no mention of fast women, but it was pretty obvious that they would have been part of his lifestyle back then.

"You sound like Lucien used to," Kara said softly.

Dylan shrugged. "Lucien is far more sorted than I ever have a hope of being. I grew up on the wrong side of the tracks, Kara. Always in scrapes, all of us, but Billy always seemed to come out of it smelling of roses. I guess I let him fool me he was okay because it was easier than asking questions." He looked back at Kara. "He got himself into all kinds of trouble. Dabbled in drugs, but gambling was his downfall. Debts up to his neck." He paused, looking down and sighing heavily. "He was my best friend, and yet he couldn't come to me when he really needed my help. What kind of a brother does that make me, Kara?" He shook his head. "Don't bother answering that."

He scrubbed his hand over his eyes. "He was found hanging. They say he did it himself, with his own belt."

Tears filled Kara's eyes as she stroked the back of Dylan's neck.

"It wasn't your fault."

"As good as," Dylan said, desolation clear in his every word. "Ignorance is no excuse. I should have been there for him, and I wasn't."

Few situations left Kara lost for words, but the injustice that Dylan had served on himself left her reeling.

"From what you've said of Billy, I'm sure he wouldn't want you to do this to yourself."

"No. He would have wanted me to save him. I'll never know for sure if he hung himself or if the bastards did it to him, and I don't know which is fucking worse anyway. He died alone and desperate, or he died terrified at the hands of someone else… either way my mother had to bury her firstborn son."

Kara brushed her fingertips tenderly over his cheeks, not sure he even knew his tears were there.

"And then there's Justin."

"Your younger brother?"

Dylan's mouth set in a grim line and the look in his eyes altered in a way that chilled Kara's bones. She saw the he didn't just dislike Justin. *He hated him.*

"You're not close?"

"He's my brother, and I never want to lay eyes on him again."

"Oh." Kara didn't want to say anything to stop him talking now he'd begun.

"Shall I tell you something really terrible?" Dylan's anguished eyes settled on Kara's, and she wasn't certain she wanted him to say his next line. Not because she feared it would change her opinion of him; rather that she feared how he'd feel after letting the dark thoughts out.

"I wish it had been him." His quiet, hollow words hung in the air. "I wish he'd been the one swinging from that fucking tree, not Billy."

Kara considered this, studying his face.

"Do you expect me to think badly of you for that?"

He half-laughed, a harsh, humourless sound. "Don't you? I just wished my baby brother dead."

"No. No you didn't. You wished that Billy wasn't dead." Kara placed her hands flat over Dylan's collarbones. "You're a good person, Dylan, but you're only human. You've lost someone you loved, and it hurts like hell."

"How do you know I'm a good person Kara? We've only known each other a couple of months. I could be anybody."

It stung to hear him diminish their relationship, and he was wrong, in part at least. They might not have known each other for a long time, but they knew each other well. It had been like the speed date that never ended since the moment she'd met him: so much intensity crammed into such a short time. Never in her life had she met a man who felt so effortlessly right. The fact that they were having this conversation while she was naked and wrapped around him on a beach was testament to that. She followed where he led, because she trusted him not to take her anywhere she didn't want to go, and she trusted him to follow her when she wanted to lead, too. She felt utterly herself with him, free to be as bold, as brazen, as womanly as she wanted.

"You're right," she said, almost exasperated. "Sure. You could be anybody. *I* could be anybody. There are no guarantees that this won't all go spectacularly wrong, but right now it feels spectacularly right to me. And to you."

Kara ran her hands over his hair and down the back of his neck.

"Spectacularly right," she whispered again, feeling him coming back towards her from the dark places in his head.

"There's other stuff I should tell you," he said, making her heart twist with the pain and vulnerability in his eyes.

"Tell me another time," she murmured. She didn't want to wring it out of him. She trusted him to tell her in his own good time. "There's no rush."

He reached out then and traced his fingers down her face.

"But…"

Kara placed a finger over his lips. "Shh. Look around us." She glanced around the tiny bay, at the glow of the fire, and then back to the incredible man beneath her. "We might never get this kind of perfect again."

Dylan's eyes tracked around as Kara's had, taking in all of the magical details. "Spectacularly right," he said softly, and she turned her mouth into his hand and kissed his palm.

The gesture was all it took to tip the emotionally charged conversation over the edge, sending it spiralling into back into the roiling deeps of desire. He gathered her against him and kissed her breathless with hot, hungry kisses that sent intense, sexual throbs shooting through her body. She didn't just want him. She needed him in a way that bordered on primal.

He shifted position when she reached for the button of his jeans, taking her with him and lying her down on her back, settling over her as he kicked his jeans off and ripped the silver foil on the condom.

She swallowed hard around the sudden ache in her throat as he positioned himself, wanting him more than she'd ever wanted anyone in her life. He paused then, lowering his head and closing his eyes to give her the slowest, sweetest of kisses as he held her hands in the cool sand beside her head.

She heard the catch in his breath as he lowered his hips down onto hers, and the answering gasp in her own as he sank himself all the way inside her. Kara felt in that moment how intense pleasure could be almost painful: so excruciatingly, mind-numbingly good that it filled every cell with a fierce yearning for more, and for sweet, sweet release.

She wrapped her arms around his broad shoulders when he let go of her hands, and they moved in slow, sacred union.

Kara opened her eyes. "I could love you, Dylan Day."

He kissed her again, open-mouthed, his hands in her hair. "I could love you too."

Lit by the firelight and bathed in the warmth of the deepest intimacy, they eased each other's weary hearts with a meander through the best cocktail menu in the world.

A supremely slow, comfortable screw.

A gasping, mind-blowing orgasm.

The most incredible sex on the beach ever.

Chapter Twenty-Six

Lucien poured wine first into Sophie's glass and then into his own, watching her as she watched the sunset. They'd discovered the laid-back beach restaurant on their last visit to the island, a sultry open air place hewn from the rock with mellow music, fabulous cocktails and great food.

"About being married, Sophie…"

She turned her attention to him, and for a second her gentle smile and the sunset gleam on her bare shoulders made him forget the conversation he wanted to initiate and contemplate taking her home to fuck her instead.

"What about it?"

He dragged himself back to the matter in hand. "I don't want it to change things."

Sophie smiled. She'd been half expecting this conversation; marriage had always been low on his agenda and she recognised that he feared what it would do to their relationship. She didn't share his fears.

"Lucien. We've been together for years. We have a child. Being married won't change any of that."

"How can you be so sure?"

"Because you won't let it, for starters."

He huffed under his breath. "I don't want to start fucking in bed with the lights off once a month."

Laughter bubbled up in Sophie's throat. "Okay. Twice a month, if you insist."

"I'm being fucking serious, Sophie. I see people get married and then, boom. It's all gone. Tedium. Mundaneness." He scowled. "Or worse."

Sophie knew what he meant, but still his thoughts amused her. Lucien wouldn't know how to be dull if he tried. He'd made the seismic shift into parenthood look easy. Being someone's husband would only serve to make him sexier still, and she intended on being an anything but routine wife.

She slipped her high heel off underneath the table and ran her bare foot up his leg and into his crotch.

"I solemnly promise not to let our marriage get dull, Lucien."

He caught hold of her ankle and massaged it, holding her foot against him. Around them, sun worshippers who'd gathered to drink cocktails and watch the sunset broke into spontaneous applause, and it took a second for Sophie to register that they were acknowledging the majesty of the sunset in the way that had become customary on the island rather than applauding her solemn promise to Lucien.

"We can write our own vows if you like," she offered, swirling her untouched wine around in her glass as she moved her toes against his hardening erection.

"Tell me more," he said, glancing downwards almost imperceptibly, meaning 'Do it more' as well.

His arm lay along the low sand-hewn wall behind him, the open sea beyond that. To anyone else in the restaurant, he looked supremely relaxed; nonchalant even, despite the fact that he was sexually aroused. Pinprick fairylights lit up the inside of the rattan ceiling like a million tiny stars, and the ethereal sound of the wind chimes dotted around underscored the low, sexy jazz music. It all came together to create a bohemian vibe, a place to let go of inhibitions and chill out.

"Well…" Sophie said, lazily rotating her foot, enjoying watching his poker face. She'd been thinking about their vows for a while. "I thought we could keep them as a surprise for each other. Kind of like a wedding present."

Lucien looked sceptical. "Are you going to promise to obey

me?"

"Do you want me to?"

"No. I quite enjoy it when you step out of line." They both fell silent for a moment, remembering the handcuffs incident in Lucien's office.

She smiled into her wine glass, then pushed it away and sipped from her tumbler of water, dragging herself back to the present. "Are *you* going to promise to obey *me*?"

"Your wish is my command, Princess. You know that already."

Sophie mulled over his light-hearted words for a while as they gazed out at the scattering of glossy, illuminated yachts anchored off the bay. He wasn't lying. He gave her everything she ever wanted and a whole lot more besides. A lifestyle way beyond anything she could have dreamt up for herself, and a love that filled every corner of her heart.

"I went for a wedding dress fitting today," she said, and he raised his eyebrows.

"Is it sexy? I like sexy."

"I know you do," she chided. "And yes, I think so. It's also a little tighter than last time."

He looked unusually perplexed, and she left him hanging for a few seconds before she spoke again, savouring the words.

"I'm pregnant, Lucien."

Sophie had grabbed a test that afternoon after trying on her bespoke wedding dress and finding her breasts uncomfortably restrained despite the careful tailoring. She watched his perplexed expression melt into a slow, incredulous, joyous smile. He dropped her ankle and slid around the alcove bench until he was beside her, one arm around her shoulders, the other cupping her face.

"Sophie... are you sure?" he said, his shining eyes searching hers. He kissed her briefly as she nodded, then lifted his head, shaking it in disbelief. "Another baby. When?"

"I'm about six weeks, I think." She dashed away a rogue tear from her lashes, unable to keep the smile from her lips.

Lucien laid his hand over her stomach, and lifted his eyes to hers.

"Are you happy?" she asked, quietly.

He lowered his eyes and drew in a long breath. "You have no idea."

Sophie stroked his cheek. "I think I do."

He looked at her untouched wine glass, and then took it from the table in front of her and dropped it into the sea behind them.

Sophie sighed. "You're not going to go all caveman on me again this time are you?" Even under usual circumstances Lucien was protective, but during her pregnancy with Tilly he'd gone into overdrive.

"Yes."

He was totally uncompromising, and she loved him all the more for it.

At the villa later that night, Lucien made slow love to Sophie until she trembled, and then slept with his head on her stomach, keeping watch over the newest love of his life.

Chapter Twenty-Seven

Dylan sat alone on the deck of the Love Tug a couple of weeks later, his eyes on the beach even though his mind was miles away. He'd tried to tell Kara the truth, he really had. The burden of lying sat heavily on his back. He'd gone over events a million times in his head, trying to make what he'd said and not said into less of a lie and more of a misunderstanding. But the plain truth was that there had been no misunderstanding. He'd invented a name because he didn't want to be the person he'd always been, because he didn't want all of the negative associations of his old life or the people in it.

He'd lied to make his own life easier, and in the process he'd made other people's lives more difficult. Lucien was lying for him, or at least covering for him. His mother was lying to anyone who asked where he'd gone. And then there was Kara.

Kara, who'd given him so much of herself and asked only one thing of him in return. Honesty.

He placed his empty beer bottle down on the table in front of him and pulled the battered brown envelope Justin had delivered towards him. Dog-eared and bent, it remained unopened, but Dylan had known all along what he'd find inside.

His stomach turned over with clammy nerves as he picked at the edge of it.

Papers.

Legal papers.

Divorce papers.

Chapter Twenty-Eight

To: mmk@toscanomail
From: mollymk@tosacanomail

Hello Matty,

Hope the job's still going well. I'm so sorry that Justin found you from my emails, I'd have warned you if I'd realised he was coming to find you. One day I'll learn my lesson. It's hard not to trust my own son.

There's something else you should know, love. Suzie was in town visiting her mother last week. Seems she's having that baby real soon, and she was asking where to find you. I didn't tell her of course, but Justin... I really hope he kept his mouth shut this time.

I'm sure it'll come to nothing, she's gone again now back to whatever hellhole she crawled out of.

Stay safe,

Mom xx

To: mollymk@toscanomail
From: mmk@toscanomail

Hi Mom,

It wasn't your fault that Justin came here, he is what he is. Just don't wait for him to change, because hand on heart I don't think it's ever going to happen.

Thanks for not telling Suzie where I am. She made her choice when she got herself pregnant with Donovan's child, and I've made my choices here in Ibiza.

I'm scared to even say it, but I'm real happy here, mom. The only thing I miss about the States is you.

Love you.
Matty

Chapter Twenty-Nine

"So, Dylan," Kara said, admiring his ass as he turned to pour them both a shot of brandy. They'd locked up and seen the last of the staff out of the building after a long, busy night. They had the whole club to themselves before the cleaning team arrived in a few hours, and they were suddenly wide awake and ready for each other's company. "A little bird tells me it's your birthday today."

Dylan slid her glass over with a roll of his eyes. "Do they now?" He didn't need to work very hard to figure out how she knew. "I might have to take a shotgun to that six foot something Norwegian little bird." Keeping things simple, he'd used his real birth date on the employment paperwork he'd filled out for Lucien all those weeks back, never thinking anyone would trouble to mark the day here on Ibiza. He'd assumed it would slide under the radar, another unwelcome link to his real life. He guessed he hadn't bargained for Lucien's eye for detail.

Kara slid off the stool, her drink in her hand. She was wearing another of her club work outfits, this time a strapless black dress that finished mid thigh and gave her a cleavage that Dylan couldn't keep his eyes off. She worked it for his benefit, wriggling her shoulders as she loosened his tie and unpopped his top button. A slow, sensual fire licked low in her gut. He looked sexily dishevelled, like the late night bartender in all the best movies.

"Come on birthday boy. Since you haven't offered me a slice of your birthday cake, I thought you might like to choose yourself a present."

"No cake," he said. "I don't want you getting a sugar rush and passing out on me."

She trailed his tie over her shoulder as she walked away, not turning because she knew he'd be behind her. She headed towards the boutique, but as they reached reception Dylan drew back, pinning her suddenly against the wall. He held her captive with his body, his hand braced on the bricks beside her head.

"The only good thing about birthdays is the kisses," he muttered into her open mouth, then kissed her hard and filthy and made her legs weak. She sank her fingernails into the firmness of his ass and yanked him deeper against her, wrapping her leg around his calf.

"I could fuck you now, right here against this wall," he whispered, putting his hand up her skirt and rubbing her through the silk of her knickers. "Rip these panties right off and slide my cock inside you." He pulled the silk to one side and pushed his fingers into her folds. He wasn't delicate, but it didn't matter because he was a man who knew exactly how to touch a woman. Who knew when to take it slow, and when to come on hard. He found her clitoris without preamble. "You like that, English? You want me to get you off?" He licked into her mouth and slid his fingers inside her, making her yelp. *Yes. Yes. Yes.*

But... *no!*

It was his birthday, and from somewhere in the recesses of her mind she dredged the recollection that she wanted to be the giver first, not the receiver. But with every nerve ending in her body wanting the orgasm he was offering her, it was a Herculean task to put the brakes on.

"Dylan..." she regretfully unwound her leg from his and pushed lightly against his chest. He lifted his head a fraction, his hand still between her legs.

"I want to give you something for your birthday first," she managed, breathless and almost boneless as his fingers stopped thrusting but carried on caressing.

"Watching you come is all I want," he whispered, playing his fingertips over her clitoris, his body up close and sensual against hers, his breath in her mouth.

She wanted to come. *Really* wanted to. She was being pinned against the wall by the man who rocked her world, and he was doing things with his fingers that were probably illegal in several countries. She'd never wanted to come that much in her entire life.

Since the last time, at least.

Dylan's eyes told her that he really wanted her to come too. They were hot, urgent and mesmerizing, locked on hers.

He pressed his weight harder against her, hitching her thighs apart with his own.

"I'll stop if you want. Just say the word."

She wanted to say the word. He licked her lips, his fingers sliding in the slick juices between her legs. She wanted to come. *No. She wanted him to come first.*

"Don't fight me, baby," he murmured, and Kara felt the beginnings of her orgasm glitter in her veins.

She didn't want to fight him. She was seconds away from not being *able* to fight him.

Stop. Don't stop. Never stop…

"Stop," she croaked, pushing him hard enough to dislodge his hand. Her body cried out for him to come back, but he nodded with a slow, quizzical look and straightened her skirt over her thighs.

"You were so close," he said, pulling her near again. "Drenched."

She moved, restless. "It's your birthday. You first."

"You English and your impeccable manners."

Kara breathed out shakily. "Trust me, Sailor. I'm right behind you in the queue."

Chapter Thirty

A couple of minutes later, Kara stood in the centre of the softly lit boutique and twirled slowly on her heel with her arms spread wide. She felt a little more in control of herself now they were on her professional territory.

"Take your pick, birthday boy. Anything you like, my treat."

"One of everything," Dylan said, not even glancing around. "Now take your dress off and let me back between your legs. My birthday, my rules. I say you come first."

Okay, maybe not quite in control.

The urge to strip and open her legs was really quite overpowering. She swallowed hard and moved to stand behind a glass counter for safety. He followed, standing in front of the counter with his head slightly to one side.

Kara looked down and tapped her fingernails on the glass, deciding what to offer him first.

He splayed his hands on the countertop, amused, ceding to her will for the moment.

"Okay. So what would you recommend, English?" His eyebrows flicked up and a lazy smile pulled at the corners of his mouth.

She reached out and slowly unknotted his tie, tugging it from around his neck as she reached into the glass cabinet for a black leather riding crop.

"Do I get to take your clothes off too?"

"Not yet." She stroked the end of the crop down her neck, closing her eyes as she moved it across the swell of her breasts.

"That would look even sexier if you lost the dress," Dylan said, his voice rich, deep and very, very interested.

Kara licked her lips, contemplating his suggestion. He was right, of course. She rounded the counter and presented her back to him, turning to glance suggestively over her shoulder. "Unzip me?"

He thought he had the upper hand, but he was dead wrong. He was coming first tonight, whether he wanted to or not. She steeled herself as his fingers brushed her back, and closed her eyes and bit her lip when his mouth lingered warm against her neck as he slid the zip all the way down to her backside. She held it in place with one arm, stepping away and turning to face him before letting it drop to the floor.

She'd dressed carefully, knowing that she wanted to seduce him. Her corset – deep ruby with black seams - cinched her waist in and pushed her breasts up, transforming her into his very own vintage dancing girl.

It didn't quite cover her breasts. It lifted them up and offered her exposed nipples to him like sweet cherries.

She licked her lips and traced the leather crop down the side of her neck again, this time drawing it down around her nipple. He tracked it with his eyes, watching her stroke herself for him.

She placed the crop in his hand and unbuttoned his shirt, trailing her nails down his skin as she went.

Then she turned to the side, placed her elbows on the glass counter, and cupped her chin delicately in her hands. Her tiny silk knickers hid nothing of the curves of her bottom.

"No one's ever spanked me before. I'd like you to be my first."

He stepped closer, and Kara jumped a little as he stroked the cheek of her ass with the crop. She wasn't lying. Spanking wasn't something that had ever happened in her sex life before.

"You would, huh?" He trailed the crop down the backs of her thighs, feather-light over the tops of her suspenders. "I'm not sure I want to mark your beautiful creamy ass," he said thoughtfully.

"Please? Just once?" she breathed. "I want to know what it feels like… and I want you to be the man who shows me."

He licked his lips. "Close your eyes, English."

She gulped, closing her eyes, her heart beating crazy fast in her chest. He ran the crop down between the cheeks of her ass, lower between her legs, over the silk there.

"You look sexy as fuck," he said, his voice thick with lust. And then he bought the crop down on her, sharp enough to make her cry out. *Fuck,* it hurt, and *fuck,* she wanted him to do it again, only harder.

"More," she whispered, and he did.

The pain was momentary, sharp, thrilling. Kara was exhilarated, high already on the endorphins, ridiculously turned on.

"Harder," she gasped, and he did. The lash fizzed white-hot across her buttocks for the third time, an exquisite sharpness that was a hair's breadth on the right side of bearable.

"Enough," he said, placing the crop down on the glass counter top, then leaning down to place a trail of hot kisses on her stinging skin. He licked lower, his tongue and hands roaming all over her ass. He'd enjoyed it too, his low groans of appreciation told her so. He was turned on as much as she was, and once more she was overwhelmed by the need to let him between her legs. He was almost there already, his teeth grazing her thighs as he dropped to his haunches behind her. And then he tilted his head and he *was* there, the barrier of her knickers ineffectual against the searing heat of his mouth. He scorched her, his tongue moving against the silk.

"Let me in, English," he said. If she did, he'd have her in seconds. She'd been ready ever since he'd slammed her against the wall in reception and put his hand up her skirt.

If it hadn't been his birthday she'd have opened her thighs and welcomed him in, but as it was, she grit her teeth and stood up, turning until he was in front of her, still on his haunches. He shook his head, laughing softly as he planted a kiss against her pubic bone and stood up too.

"You *will* come before I do," he said as he shook his shirt off his shoulders.

Kara laughed, shaking her head slowly, raising one delicate shoulder as she dropped her eyes and played with her nipples. She was going to win this battle. She counted to five before raising her gaze again, giving him time to really appreciate watching her touch herself.

She stepped away from him, running her fingers over the shelves as she decided on his next birthday gift.

"There are so many things I'd like to give you," she said. He didn't take his eyes off her.

She picked up a large, deep purple vibrator. "This maybe?" She slid her hands down the shaft. "Would you like to fuck me with this, Sailor?"

He stepped closer, and she noticed the harsh movement of his Adam's apple as he swallowed.

"Because I'd like you to," she said, running the tactile rubber down her stomach and between her legs.

Dylan's lips parted slightly, his eyes molten as he took the vibrator from her fingers and placed it on the counter behind them beside the crop.

"Another time, baby," he whispered, dragging her against him. "Tonight I need to fuck you properly." His fingers explored the stinging cheeks of her ass as he kissed her. She relished the heat of her buttocks under his palms. "Feel what you've done to me, Kara." His erection strained hard against her.

She reached down between them and massaged him, making him groan.

"I think you're ready for a special present."

She slid his zip down and pushed her hand inside. Her stomach turned somersaults as her fingers curled around him, iron hard silk as he rocked himself in her hand.

She had him naked within seconds.

"Do you trust me, Dylan?" she whispered against his ear,

working his shaft slowly.

"Right now? With my life," he groaned, fondling her breasts.

She reached for his discarded tie. "Good." She led him to sit on a high backed chair and covered his eyes with his tie, knotting it behind his head.

"English…"

"You trust me, remember?"

She stood for a second and gathered a couple of items, then returned to stand behind him. She leaned down, her bare breasts brushing his shoulder. "What shall I do with you, Dylan?" she said against his ear, sliding her palms down his chest.

"I've taken off my knickers. I could sit astride you, take your cock all the way inside me." She slipped her hand lower to pump his shaft a little. "Should I do that, do you think?"

He turned and caught her mouth with his own.

"Yes, Kara. Yes. You should do that." He reached for her and she dodged his hands. If he caught her now it would all be over. She'd straddle him, and he'd make her come, and it would be incredible… but she had other plans, and she was sticking to them.

Picking up her chosen sex toy from the floor, she knelt in front of him and placed it in his hands, spreading his knees to sit between them.

"What the hell is this thing?"

"Shhh," she said, and licked the length of his shaft.

"Fuck."

She opened her mouth and took him inside.

"Fuck…"

He was so very hard, and it was so very tempting to keep going. He'd come, she'd win, and then he'd make her come and she'd win all over again.

But today was his birthday, and she wanted to give him an experience that no one else had ever given him before.

So she took the toy from his hands, a skin-warm, slim silicon oval designed to pleasure him. It hinged open to reveal supple, textured rollers that would close around him like lips. She flipped it wide, lubricated it, then closed it around the base of his cock, making him jerk with surprise.

"Easy," she murmured. "You have no idea how filthy you look right now. I so want to grab my phone and take a picture." She gripped the silicon oval at either end and moved it slowly up his cock, watching the rollers clasp and massage his shaft as she moved it up and down.

"Fucking hell…" he moaned.

The toy was one of their newest and most expensive items, and judging by Dylan's pleasure, it was worth every penny. Designed for couple play, it left the majority of his cock free to lick, suck and fondle, and Kara took full advantage. She rolled it up and down the length of him, following it closely with her mouth. Dylan moaned, his hands in her hair, sometimes stroking, sometimes pressing her down on him.

Kneeling cross-ankled between his thighs in the middle of the boutique was another memory she committed to the forever vault, and as he shoved the tie up off his face to watch her, his frenetic movements told her that he'd let go of his control.

She twisted the toy in her hands, giving him new sensations even as his hips spasmed, and seconds later her name ripped from his chest as his salty semen hit the back of her throat.

Looking up at him in those moments, a profound sense of rightness settled on her shoulders. He looked overwhelmed. She'd given him that. She'd put that look of intense pleasure on his face.

She loved this man.

"You give the best birthday presents," he said, his hand lazy in her hair, his other arm dropping towards the floor. "What is that thing anyway?"

She removed the toy and put it to one side.

"Did you like it?"

"I'm kind of glad I was blindfolded," he admitted, eying it dubiously.

"Yeah, yeah. But did you like it?"

"Sure. I liked it." A languid, lopsided smile tipped his lips. "It felt fucking amazing."

Kara nodded. "So I can tell our customers that the boss endorses it?"

"Not a chance."

She smiled, standing up and and crossing to the counter to gather his gifts together. The leather crop. The purple vibrator. The slender oval masturbator that she planned on using on him again some time very soon.

Dylan moved to stand behind Kara, sweeping her hair over one shoulder and lowering his mouth to the warm curve of her neck. He breathed her in deep. The familiar, clean scent of her hair, the delicate perfume she always used. His tiny bathroom on the boat smelled of her, as did his bedsheets. She surrounded him.

"You lied to me," he said against her ear. "You're still wearing your panties." He ran his hand under the slim band of silk on her hip.

"Knickers," she corrected, aware of his naked body against hers.

"And you made me come," he said, cupping her breasts, his cock stirring against the softness of her behind as her nipples hardened in his fingers.

"It *is* your birthday," she said, leaning her head back on his shoulder.

"It is." Not such a bad thing to have been found out after all, Dylan reflected.

They stood for a second, caught up in each other, Dylan savouring the feel of Kara's responsive body in his hands, Kara savouring the feel of Dylan's questing hands on her body.

He moved then, returning a moment later with his jeans tugged on and his shirt in his hands.

"Put this on. There's something we need to do."

"Let's do it here," she said, not wanting to do anything that didn't involve his hands between her legs.

He laughed under his breath. "Just put the shirt on, English. I'll make it worth the wait."

He helped her into his shirt, and gathered their belongings in his arms before leading her out through the club. He flicked the alarms on as he locked up, then led Kara out to the Mustang, the only car left on the small staff parking lot.

Dylan deposited their stuff on the driver's seat.

"I've fantasised about this for days, English," he murmured, lifting her lightly and sitting her on the folded-back material of the convertible roof. He swung himself over the edge of the car to kneel in front of her on the back bench seat, implausibly sexy and shirtless by moonlight.

"My shirt looks good on you," he said, opening it to reveal her breasts to his waiting eyes and mouth.

"I might keep it forever," she said, bracing her hands behind her, letting the material slide back on her shoulders as he licked the sensitive undersides of her breasts. She sighed a little when his hand moved to touch her between her legs.

"This feels like the best teenage date ever," she said, breathless as he pulled her knickers to the side.

"The girls back home never looked like you do right now," he said, and slid his fingers all the way inside her.

Kara gasped down a big lungful of the balmy Spanish night air.

"The boys back home never made me feel the way you do right now," she managed to say. Just.

The idea of anyone else touching Kara like this triggered his kill instinct for a few seconds.

"Thank fuck for that."

Dylan hunkered down and buried his head between her legs, his mouth hot all over her.

She tasted sweet as sugar, of longing, and of frustration, the best birthday surprise he'd ever had.

He let his eyes roam up over her curves as he tasted her, over her swells and her hollows, and his heart contracted.

He loved this woman.

Kara leaned her head back and looked up at the stars. He had her spread wide, exposed and vulnerable, yet she'd never felt as safe and secure with anyone in her life. Dylan drew her clitoris into the heat of his mouth and took his time over making sure that even when she'd buried her hands in his hair and screwed her eyes tight shut to absorb the bone-drenching pleasure, she could still see stars.

Chapter Thirty-One

Sophie opened her eyes slowly. Dawn sunlight shafted through the gauze curtains onto Lucien, turning her sleeping Viking into a fallen angel.

Today was the day she'd become his wife. His fingers were curled loosely around hers as he slept and she tightened her grip on them as she closed her eyes again, thanking her lucky stars for the love of the best man in the world.

Aboard the Love Tug, Dylan stirred. Kara slept beside him tangled in the white cotton sheets, her skin lustrous gold from a summer spent working and playing beneath the Spanish sunshine. The sun had added blonde streaks to her tawny waves too, and to Dylan's eyes she surpassed any of the surf-streaked Californian beach beauties back home.

Back home. Dylan frowned at the thought. California didn't feel like home anymore. His home was here in Ibiza now, but he knew that for Kara it had always been intended as a temporary arrangement, a secondment for a few months over the summer while the boutique established itself under local management. She had a whole life to return to back in England: family, friends. Sophie and Lucien too, because they'd be heading back to the UK a couple of weeks after the wedding.

It was all ending. He'd let himself live the lie for long enough, had kept awarding himself an extra roll of the dice to give himself more time as Dylan Day, more time in this gilded bubble of pleasure with Kara.

He'd allow the dice roll to in his favour as far as the wedding, but then that was it. No more. He'd stand beside Lucien as his best man, he'd dance with the most beautiful bridesmaid he'd ever lay eyes on, and then he'd confess his dark secrets and let the chips fall where they will.

Chapter Thirty-Two

"Champagne for the bride," Kara carried two full flutes into Sophie's bedroom, dressed in a cream silk slip with her hair wound around velcro rollers. She set one glass of bucks fizz down on Sophie's dressing table and sipped from the other. "Don't worry, yours is mostly orange juice," she grinned. "How are you doing?"

"Good," Sophie raised her glass with a smile a mile wide.

"This is probably the coolest wedding ever," Kara said happily. "Hardly any guests, sand under your toes, and champagne on tap."

Sophie sipped her fizz. "Yeah, well, I did the big dress and party number last time around, remember?"

This was the second time that Kara had been Sophie's bridesmaid. She made a rueful face, casting her mind back for a moment to Sophie's wedding to Dan, her first husband. It all seemed so long ago now, and they'd all done a lot of growing up since those days.

"Jeez, remember your mum? She was practically hysterical by the time the wedding day actually arrived. Thank God you're getting married while they're not around," Kara said. "I don't think she'd be able to stand it all over again. Especially with it being shot-gun, and all." Her mock-scandalised gaze dropped dramatically to the almost imperceptible swell of Sophie's tummy.

Sophie laughed. Kara had a point. Her mother had no desire to reprise her role as mother of the bride; she'd found it terribly stressful first time around, almost as stressful as she'd found her only daughter's divorce. Lucien had of course charmed her parents completely in the intervening years; even her father seemed to enjoy his son-in-law's company. They all got along like a house on fire, under the tacit understanding that no one mentioned Lucien's line of business under any circumstances. Her parents liked to consider themselves liberal, just as long as no one used the 'sex' word.

Still, they'd been thrilled to hear about the wedding plans, delighted to hear about the new baby, and ecstatic at the thought of throwing a small wedding party at the golf club when they were all back in England in a few weeks time. At this precise moment, Sophie's parents were enjoying a long-anticipated cruise, and the timing could not have been more fortuitous for all concerned.

"Yes, I think it's worked out pretty well for everyone," Sophie agreed.

She eyed herself in the mirror. In just a few hours she would finally become Lucien's wife. The fact that she'd been someone's wife before hadn't even figured in her thoughts in the days leading up to the wedding, because this felt brand new. Being Mrs. Knight would bear absolutely no relation to the time she'd spent as Mrs. Black.

In truth, being Mrs. Knight was a unique proposition: their relationship hadn't followed any of the conventional patterns and she had no doubt that their marriage would be all the stronger for it. They knew each other so very well now.

Behind her, her ivory wedding dress hung on the wardrobe door. Raw silk tulle overlaid with a cobweb-fine layer of beaded vintage Spanish lace, the delicate empire line dress shimmered with nineteen-twenties glamour. Sheer capped sleeves and a gracefully scooped v neckline made the very best of her pregnancy bloom, highlighting the swell of her breasts and skimming over the new curves of her abdomen. It made her feel like a million dollars, a film star for the day.

"Come on Juliet," Kara said, putting her already half empty glass down and starting to unravel Sophie's hair from her rollers. "Let's get you ready for your Romeo."

Sophie caught her friend's eye in the mirror, her own expression merry.

"You do know how that ended, right?"

Kara tittered. "Imagine that. You and Mr. K." She drew her finger across her throat dramatically.

Sophie arched her eyebrows and reached for her champagne flute.

"If we're talking star-crossed lovers, how about we get onto you and delicious Dylan?"

Sophie didn't miss the way Kara's face softened at the mention of his name.

"I can't believe I've only known him a few months," Kara said. Then, more seriously, "Is it too fast, Soph?"

Sophie laughed softly. "There isn't a rule book, Kara. You could spend your whole life looking and never find anything close to how you feel now ever again. You remember how it was for me with Lucien? He came out of the blue and totally blindsided me. It was like love on fast forward, and look at us now. Look at us today."

Kara nodded, drawing in a deep breath.

"I... I love him."

"I know you do," Sophie said, as if Kara had just told her that the sun rose in the east. "And I know he loves you right back."

"How can you know?"

Sophie sighed. What was it about love that it could make nervy, moonstruck teenagers out of two usually confident, self-assured adults?

"Because it's written all over his face every time you're in the same room. He can't take his eyes off you."

A slow tingle of happiness ran deliciously through Kara's body. She knew that Sophie was right. She could feel Dylan's love all around her, and it was time for them to act like grown ups and talk about it. This wasn't like all the other times in her life. He wasn't like Richard, some selfish prick living two lives just so he could have his cake and eat it. He wasn't like her father, someone who always put his own happiness first at the expense of the people who loved him.

He was Dylan-fucking-yankee-doodle-Day, resident of the floating shag palace, world-class kisser, and the owner of her heart.

"I'm going to tell him tonight."

"Well, you picked a good day for it." Sophie's eyes shone over-bright as she met Kara's in the mirror before her.

"The best, Soph." Kara squeezed Sophie's shoulder then laughed a little, breaking the emotional charge.

"Now pull yourself together, you daft cow. Those baby hormones have a lot to answer for."

Chapter Thirty-Three

Sometimes, very rarely, there are perfect days in our lives. Sometimes they happen unexpectedly, they start out normal and then something happens to make them burn brightly in our memories forever. And sometimes they happen because there's no way they could be anything *but* perfect, because they are so jammed full of special moments that thinking back over them warms our hearts even on the coldest of days.

Lucien and Sophie's wedding was always going to be one of those days.

The afternoon sky seemed a little bluer and the sun a little brighter to Sophie as she stepped out of the villa with Kara and Tilly at her side. She'd grinned with delight as she'd dressed her daughter in her meltingly gorgeous white cotton bridesmaid dress, every inch her daddy's little girl with her blonde locks and his blue steel eyes.

Sophie saw in Tilly the child that Lucien must have been, precocious and funny, as happy to run in the arctic snow as she was to play on an Ibizan beach. Already well travelled, Tilly was destined to grow up a cosmopolitan young woman with the world at her feet. Sophie pitied her boyfriends in decades to come; it was hard to imagine a more formidably protective father than Lucien. She imagined the boys quailing under his gaze. He was protective of all of them. Of Sophie, and Tilly, and of the unborn child who had already begun to weave its gossamer thread into the fabric of their family.

She turned as Kara squeezed her elbow, beautiful beside her

in a bias cut, calf length nude pink dress that suited her sun-kissed complexion perfectly.

"Time to go," Kara said, propelling her gently forward towards the waiting car.

"I know," Sophie said softly, breathing in the scent of the wild flowers she held, a larger version of the corsage on Kara's wrist and the tiny posy clutched in Tilly's hand. She kissed her daughter's apple cheek as Esther, her nanny, appeared and scooped her into her arms to go and secure her in the car.

Sophie stilled on the steps and turned to Kara.

"Don't you dare start crying," Kara warned. "Lucien is expecting radiant, not the bride of Dracula. I'm not bringing any fresh mascara."

"I'm not going to cry," Sophie said. "Not yet, anyway."

She looked out beyond the villa at the lush Ibizan landscape. "This place has been good to all of us, hasn't it?"

Kara nodded, suddenly nostalgic even though the summer wasn't quite at its end. The day was heavy with portentous, magical romance, of lifetime love being sealed with a promise, and of precious new love being acknowledged for the first time.

Despite her stern warning to Sophie, tears lodged in her own throat and she resolutely swallowed them down.

"Come on, lady. We need to get you to the beach on time."

Dylan drove Lucien to the secluded private cove in Kara's red Mustang, roof down, shades on, a whole lot of handsome that turned the head of every woman they passed along the way.

Lucien's perfectly tailored black-blue suit followed close against the lines of his body, his open necked white shirt an elegant contrast with his golden skin. He epitomised laid-back glamour in the way only a beautiful, self assured man can.

At the wheel, Dylan was a different kind of sexy. A little more subtle maybe, a little less intense, yet no less capable of commanding any room he walked into. They made a formidable duo as Dylan parked the car at the top of the cove, flicking his phone onto silent when it buzzed for the third time since they'd set out. He wasn't in work mode today.

"I'm guessing there's no need to say it's not too late to back out," he said with a grin, getting out of the car and running his hand over his inside pocket for the tenth time since that morning. Yes, the rings were still there. "You'd have to be one crazy fool to *not* marry someone like Sophie."

Lucien rested against the side of the car, his arms crossed lightly over his chest. His tone was thoughtful.

"I used to think you'd have to be a crazy fool to marry anyone."

Dylan looked out across the still, blue sea, keeping his personal feelings towards marriage firmly out of the conversation.

"So what changed?"

Lucien shrugged. "I still think everyone *else* is a crazy fool to do it."

"But not you?"

"Hell, yeah. I'm as much of a crazy fool for Sophie as the next guy. Whatever love is, it's what I have with her."

Around them, the sounds of nature filled the quiet air. The chirp of crickets, the light breeze moving through the leaves, the distant lap of the Mediterranean.

"From where I'm standing, that makes you lucky, not crazy."

"Crazy *and* lucky. I can live with that."

The cherry red Mustang was conspicuous when the car bearing Sophie and Kara eased into the tiny clearing that served as the beach car park.

"Looks like you haven't been stood up at the altar," Kara said lightly, glad to be able to be flippant about a subject that a few months previously would have wounded her deeply. As they stepped onto the sand, she straightened Sophie's train and made last minute adjustments to her artfully romantic up-do, checking that the tiny fresh flowers she'd pinned in the back of it still looked perfect.

A single diamond on a golden trace chain glittered at Sophie's throat, a wedding gift from Lucien. The bracelet around her wrist was her only other jewellery, another gift from Lucien, given to her back when he hadn't known how to express his love in words. He'd shown her instead by entrusting his mother's bracelet into her care, one of his most treasured possessions, and now one of hers.

A slow, steady bloom of joy unfurled inside Sophie's chest as she and Kara picked their way along the path towards the beach, Tilly scampering ahead of them.

The late afternoon sun hung low in the sky, casting the whole scene peachy gold. The tiny, private cove provided the perfect, intimate setting for this most special of days, with its sugar-white sands and a tiny pavilion restaurant nestled at the edge. The soft, joyful sound of steel drum music floated on the air as Kara caught up with Tilly and took her hand. She shook it off and set off purposefully across the deeper sand, wobbly and ungainly but determined, making Sophie and Kara laugh as they clutched each other's forearms to kick their shoes off.

In the distance, a raffia pergola stood close to the sea's edge, fresh island flowers wound around its struts.

Inside it were three figures. The wedding celebrant. Dylan.

And Lucien.

Sophie stopped for a second and caught her breath as she looked at him, so distinctive even from a distance. He turned at the sound of Tilly running towards him, breaking into a huge smile and hunkering down with his arms out towards the little girl. Sophie watched him swing her up into his arms, and whoosh, her heart burst wide with love for them both. Kara gripped her hand tight.

"I hope I have what you have one day, Sophie."

Sophie hugged her quickly. "You will, Kara."

Sophie saw Dylan turn and raise his hand in greeting across the beach.

"You might just have found it already."

Chapter Thirty-Four

Lucien walked to meet them a little way before they reached the pergola, handing Tilly over to Kara as she moved away to join Dylan.

"You look so much beyond beautiful," he said softly when they were alone, and Sophie found herself breathless and close to tears. He'd never looked more handsome, and the rare edge of vulnerability in his eyes made her heart swell with love for him. He'd laid aside all of his fears and prejudices against marriage for her, long held beliefs that had crumbled in the face of their big, huge, unconditional love for each other.

"You too, Lucien," she said, reaching out to lay her palm on his cheek.

He turned his face into her hand and kissed it. "You ready?"

She laughed gently. "I've been ready since the first day I met you, Lucien Knight."

He leaned down and lifted her in his arms. "You're supposed to do this *after* we're married," she said, looping her arms around his neck as he walked towards the pergola.

"When did we ever do things the conventional way?" he said, his fingers finding the hidden zip at the side of her dress.

"Lucien…"

"Just checking for later," he murmured against her hair, depositing her on her bare feet beneath the raffia canopy, then dropping a kiss on her forehead. "Come on, Princess. Let's do this thing."

Kara sat down facing the ocean with Tilly sitting on her knees and Dylan alongside her with his arm slung across the back of her chair. In front of them, the celebrant began the informal ceremony, welcoming them to witness the marriage of Sophie and Lucien. A tingle ran down Kara's spine as she listened to the words, and for the first time ever she silently thanked Richard for standing her up at the altar.

This was a real wedding. *This* was true love. Lucien and Sophie stood in front of her, facing each other, and no one else existed in their world at that moment.

Sophie looked down at Lucien's hands holding her smaller ones, his thumbs gentle over her knuckles as the celebrant asked if there was anything she'd like to say to Lucien before she gave him his ring. She nodded and swallowed hard. There was so much she wanted to say.

"Lucien." She looked into his beautiful eyes and stepped close. He held on tight to her hands. "You've taught me that love is so much bigger than I ever knew it could be." She paused, gathering herself together. "I love you for so many different reasons. For your generosity and your spirit, for your loyalty and your strength, and for your vulnerability. I love you because you let me in." She couldn't keep the catch from her voice, and his eyes burned over-bright with emotion.

"I promise to love you forever, with every breath in my body." She smiled, and then added under her breath, for his ears alone, "More than once a month with the lights out."

He laughed softly and looked at the floor, nodding.

"You made me into the princess from all of the fairy tales I loved as a child, Lucien," she said, and when he looked up at her again his eyes told her he loved her in a million different ways.

"I love you for the man you've always been, for the father you've become, and for the husband you're going to be."

She took his ring from the celebrant's outstretched palm.

"Lying with you beneath the northern lights, or here beneath the Spanish sun… you're my Viking and my sunshine." The tears ran unchecked down her cheeks now. "You're my hero, Lucien Knight."

She slid the ring onto his wedding finger, holding it there for a few seconds, sealing it forever with her love.

"Always, Lucien. Always."

Behind them, Dylan rubbed Kara's shoulder, seeing the happy tears glittering on her cheeks as she cradled Tilly in her arms. He knew without question that he wanted her in his life forever, and he knew with almost as much certainty that he was going to lose her.

Lucien breathed in hard as Sophie slipped the ring on his finger. He hadn't counted on the amazing sense of peace that seeing it there would bring him, or that he'd finally, *finally* understand the reason why people all around the world of all different faiths wedded themselves to each other forever. Why they placed their blind faith in someone else, and their heart in someone else's hands, and trusted them not to break it into smithereens.

He drew Sophie close, her face in his hands, and kissed her mouth. Her lips were warm and pliant, salty with her tears.

"I think you're supposed to wait until the end to do that," she whispered, laughing shakily. As if Lucien was ever going to follow the rules.

The celebrant held his palm out, and Lucien took Sophie's ring between his fingers with the reverence it deserved. And then he looked up at Sophie with all of the devotion she deserved, too.

"Sophie," he said, and wiped the tears from her cheek with his fingertips. "There isn't a single part of my life that isn't a hundred times better for having you in it." He wanted to remember the look on her face forever. "You're the girl who kisses envelopes before you mail them," he said. "The girl who still surprises me every single day. The world's a better place through your eyes than mine." He stroked the back of his fingers along her jawline.

"Before you, I thought I was a lone wolf. I was wrong. I need my pack. You. Tilly." He laid his hand on her stomach. "This baby. All the important lessons in life I've learned have been from you. You've shown me that love doesn't have to break people."

Reaching for her left hand, he stroked his thumb over the place her ring would fit.

"I promise to love you forever, Sophie, and to honour every perfect inch of your body with my own. Often. Daily. Sometimes twice a day," he added. Behind them, Kara and Dylan's soft laughter carried on the breeze.

"I promise I'll never leave you, or screw anyone else, or break your heart." He slid the ring onto her wedding finger and knew he'd never seen anything as profoundly perfect in his life. Sophie gasped softly, tears on her cheeks all over again.

"I look at you today, barefoot and beautiful, growing our baby inside you, and I wonder how the hell I got this lucky." He moved her in close, sliding his arm around her waist and lifting her hand to his mouth. He placed his lips over her wedding ring and set the seal.

"You're *my* fucking hero, Sophie Knight."

They danced as the sun set over this most blissful of days.

Encircled in Lucien's arms, Sophie laid her head on his shoulder and let her gaze slide slowly over the scene as he stroked her back. Tilly, crashed out on a cream, calico-covered lounger that had appeared out of nowhere just when it was needed.

Kara and Dylan, their arms wrapped around each other. Sophie could see Dylan's face as he rested his chin on top of Kara's head, and his expression told her all she needed to know about the depth of his feelings for the woman in his arms.

She breathed in a deep, happy sigh and closed her eyes, wondering if she'd ever experience such a perfect moment again.

Lucien Knight.

Her love, her hero, and finally, her husband.

Chapter Thirty-Five

Kara and Dylan made their way home in the Mustang a couple of hours later. He slung his arm around her waist, her sandals hanging from his fingers as they walked slowly along the beach towards the Love Tug, close enough to the water's edge for the sea to wash over Kara's bare feet.

"That was, hands down, the best wedding I've ever been to," she said, winding both of her arms around Dylan's midriff. It had been the most impossibly romantic of days, and she was ready now to tell the man at her side that she loved him.

He kissed the top of her head. "Starry-eyed fool."

Kara wriggled her toes in the shallow water. "I used to be." She stilled, smooched him a little. Warm mouths, soft sighs. "Still starry-eyed. But not a fool anymore," she said. "I picked you."

Dylan's conviction to tell her the truth dissolved in her kiss. He let himself roll the dice one last time. It had been the best of days. Let tonight be the best of nights, and come morning he'd tell Kara everything.

They were good plans. Great, even. Brave courses set for the best of reasons. But what neither of them had factored in was the vulnerability of their plans to outside interference. As they strolled up the beach, both spotted the lone figure ahead at the same moment.

For Kara, there was no moment of instant horror and panic, but for Dylan there most definitely was as the man drew himself up to standing as they approached the pathway.

Dylan's fingers bit suddenly into Kara's waist, her first warning that something was amiss.

"About time too," the man said, a triumphant grin on his face as his sly gaze moved between Kara and Dylan.

"What the fuck…?" Dylan ground out. Kara felt her world tip a little at his expression, at the rage in his voice.

"I told you never to come back here," Dylan said, his voice low and full of menace as he stepped protectively in front of Kara.

"Extenuating circumstances, bro." Justin shrugged his shoulders with the look of a man who knows he's holding an ace.

Fear spiked through Dylan's heart as he remembered turning off his phone earlier that day. Had Justin been trying to reach him? *Had something happened to their mother?*

Kara stood stock still, her mind reeling. *Bro?* This was Justin? This was Dylan's surviving brother? There was little to link them, aside from their familiar accents and maybe their eyes. She made up her mind within seconds that Justin was a man with none of his brother's virtues.

She placed her hand on Dylan's arm as he moved threateningly towards the other man.

"Dylan…" she murmured, and Justin looked her straight in the eyes and laughed.

"Dylan?" He rolled his eyes. "Fuck, man!"

Dylan had his brother by the scruff of the neck within a second and had him pinned against the rocks.

"Don't you fucking dare," he growled. "Not like this."

Kara's world tilted even more queasily to the side. *There was something very, very wrong.* Dylan drew his fist back, but it stilled in mid air as Justin inclined his head towards someone new approaching the tense gathering. Kara swung around too, and they all watched as a woman headed towards them, stumbling awkwardly as she dragged a pushchair through the deep sand. Tall and skinny, her dark hair was pulled back in a tight ponytail, her cotton dress was rumpled, and the tight, resentful look on her face spelled even more trouble.

"So you finally decided to show up," she drawled, her eyes on Dylan as she came close to them.

Kara wrapped her arms around her midriff, an instinctively protective stance. She couldn't speak. The look on Dylan's face had again taken her breath. Whoever this woman was, she was no stranger to him.

Silence reigned for a few long seconds as the woman's gaze shifted from Dylan to Kara.

"Looks like it's down to me to make the introductions, darlin'," she said, her eyebrows raised over her bitterly triumphant eyes.

Dylan let Justin go with a shove and turned to Kara. The look on his face broke her heart clean in two. Her world was about to turn upside down. She knew it in that split second as she waited mutely to hear what Dylan – or the woman - would say.

"Kara, please…"

"Oh, this is gonna be fuckin' priceless," Justin laughed. Without a second's hesitation, Dylan swung around and punched him so hard on the jaw that he fell to his knees. Kara flinched, as much for the anguished, animal sound that left Dylan's body when the blow struck its target as for the sound of knuckles smashing against bone.

"Some things never change, Matthew," the woman said coolly, watching with apparent disinterest as Justin staggered to his feet, swiping blood from his mouth on the back of his hand.

Dylan's heart was beating hard enough to give him a coronary. *It wasn't supposed to end like this.*

"Kara…" he said, hating the hunted look in her eyes and wanting like hell to hold her.

"She called you Matthew," Kara whispered, her face ashen even in the moonlight. "Why did she call you Matthew?"

The woman's eyes widened and a small laugh escaped her throat.

"Oh my God," she said, amused, furious, dangerous beyond reason. "She doesn't even know your fucking name."

"Shut the fuck up, Suzie," Dylan said, never taking his eyes off Kara. He reached for her hands but she stepped backwards, out of his reach.

"Who is she?" Kara demanded, terrified of hearing his answer.

Suzie didn't shut the fuck up. She stepped up alongside Dylan instead and stuck her hand out. Kara stared at it dumbly.

"I'm Suzie, honey," she said, retracting her hand with a shrug, laying it on Dylan's bicep instead. "His wife." She glanced sideways and waved her other hand towards the pushchair. "And that's his son."

Chapter Thirty-Six

Kara ran. She ran barefoot across the beach, as fast as she could without looking back. She heard Dylan call her name, once, and then again closer behind her. He caught her easily, his arms banding around her midriff, holding her against his chest as she struggled, throwing her elbows back into his body as hard and viciously as she could.

"Let me go," she panted, fighting against him with every ounce of strength in her.

"She's not my wife, Kara," he said desperately, still holding her tight. "Not any more, I swear to you."

She stilled in his grasp, winded by his words. He let go slowly, as if he feared she was preparing to run again. But she wasn't. She didn't want to run, suddenly. She wanted to hit him, to hurt him, to give him even the smallest taste of how much he was hurting her at that moment.

"But she *was* your wife, and you just conveniently forgot to mention her," she spat. "I only ever asked you for one thing, Dylan." She laughed, acid-harsh, as she said his name. "Or Matthew. Which is it?" She shook her head, and the icy revulsion in her eyes chilled his bones. "I only ever asked you for honesty."

"I wanted to tell you, Kara," he said hopelessly. "I wanted to tell you more than anything."

"Well, you had plenty of fucking opportunities," she threw back. "Months. Months of working alongside me, of screwing me all over this goddamn island, of listening to me spill my guts to you about fucking Richard, and my fucking dad." She was crying now, big, heavy sobs dragging on her chest that made talking hard, but the words kept tumbling out regardless. "You really saw me coming, didn't you?"

In the distance, the baby cried out.

"You're not the man I thought you were," Kara said, her voice broken and quiet. "I was going to tell you that I love you tonight. That I wanted to stay with you forever on that fucking boat."

Dylan stared at her, hating himself, loving her so much it physically hurt. He could feel himself losing her and nothing he could say was going to make her stay.

"You're someone else's husband, and you let me fall in love with you," Kara said. "She has your baby, and you pretend it's never happened and let me fall in love with you."

"It's not my baby," he whispered.

"You expect me to believe that?" Her eyes were daggers.

He didn't. "Kara, we're divorced. I have the papers on the boat…" Raw desperation hollowed his voice. He reached out for her and she backed away, shaking her head vehemently.

"I don't want your papers, or your lies, or your fucking hands on me ever again." Her voice shook with rage. "You make me feel dirty."

It was the hardest thing anyone had ever said to him. She carried on retreating, watching him like a wounded animal, her furious face telling him how much she didn't want him to follow. "I don't know who you are," she said flatly, a few metres away from him now. "I don't know who you are." She pressed her hands against her cheeks. Shock was setting in. She was cold, shivering despite the warmth of the evening.

"Yes you do," he said softly, desperate to touch her, knowing she didn't want him to. "You know me better than anyone else has ever known me." He glanced back up the beach. "I don't belong with them, Kara. I belong here, with you. I love you."

For the briefest of seconds he saw her falter, and hope flared bright in his heart. Would she stop? Would she come back? The truth was so dreadfully overdue, but he would tell it all, right now, if she gave him the chance. *Please come back.*

Pain etched lines across her forehead as she fought to make sense of the evening's revelations, to pick the bones of truth out from amongst the lies.

Kara had made her mind up.

"Go." she said, clearly. "Go back to your family." She jerked her head towards the end of the beach, her expression determined. "I never want to see you again."

Dylan watched her walk away, taking his heart with her. He didn't try to stop her. How could he? He had no defence.

Every word she'd said was true. He *had* lied to her from the moment he'd met her. He *had* chosen not to take a single one of the many opportunities there had been to tell her the truth.

He watched her walk towards the Mustang, heard the hard slam of the door reverberate across the beach, stood bone still until he saw the tail lights had climbed the hill and disappeared around the curve of the road.

She was gone, and he was left there holding her silvery sandals, Prince Charming without his Cinderella. Except he wasn't the hero. He was the villain, the liar, the man who always lost in the end. He turned away and walked slowly towards the two people he hated most in the world, and the child he'd never laid his eyes on in his life.

Chapter Thirty-Seven

Every dread-filled step back along the beach towards Justin and Suzie was a step back into his old shoes. He could feel Dylan Day dissolving into the Ibizan sand beneath his feet, leaving him exposed as Matthew McKenzie, the man who let his brother die.

"Leave us," he snarled at Justin as he approached them. Justin shrank back into the shadows, presumably not wishing to have his face rearranged for a second time that evening.

Suzie sat on the rocks, disinterestedly feeding the baby in the pushchair in front of her from a plastic bottle.

Dylan sighed heavily and sat down a couple of feet away from her, his head in his hands. The sea washed unnoticed over his shoes.

"What the fuck is going on here, Suzie?" he said eventually.

She looked across at him. She looked worn out, more jaded than the last time he'd seen her.

"This *is* your kid."

She set the baby's almost empty bottle down on the rocks and reached into the pushchair to lean him forward, rubbing his back, his chin resting between her thumb and forefinger as she winded him. Dylan stared at him, his tiny face and startling mop of dark hair. *How could that be his son?*

"I was pregnant when I left you." Suzie answered the question he hadn't yet asked. She continued patting mechanically, not looking at the baby, her attention on Dylan.

"Yeah, and you'd been screwing Donovan for months before then," Dylan reminded her, certain that he hadn't fathered the child.

He'd barely had sex with Suzie in the last few months of their doomed-from-the-start marriage. Just once or twice, and unhappily, thanks to too much tequila when he'd been especially maudlin about Billy.

The discovery that Suzie had been screwing around behind his back had come as no great surprise. They'd married in Vegas not long after Billy had died, and neither of them had much recollection of the ceremony or of their reasons behind it. Billy had been their link. His brother, her ex-lover. He'd tried to lie in the bed he'd made for a while, but the truth was that it had been a cold and hard place. Numbed by so much unhappiness, he hadn't been one bit sorry to see her pack her bags.

Suzie had been a symptom rather than the cause. It hadn't even hurt that she'd left him to shack up with Donovan, the very guy to whom both of his brothers had gambled their lives away to, the very same guy who had taken everything Dylan owned beside the shirt on his back in recompense for Justin's unpaid debts. It had been a stark choice. His club, or his brother. The fact that his wife had thrown herself into the equation too barely even registered. He'd made the choice he wished he'd been able to make for Billy. He did it *for* Billy, and to save his mother from the heartache of burying another son.

"He's been tested," Suzie said, nodding down at the baby. "He's not Donovan's. He even looks like a fucking McKenzie."

Dylan digested her words, every one a death knell for him.

"So what… you've come here after money?" Dylan guessed. "If he's my child then you know I'll pay."

"I don't want your money," she said. "And I don't want your child, either."

He jerked his head up, not understanding, and she shrugged.

"Come on, Matthew. Do you really think Donny's going to raise a McKenzie brat?"

It had been a long night. Given time to absorb the facts and think about it, Dylan wouldn't have wanted Donovan anywhere near his son either. But as it was, in his state of numb shock, he needed her to spell things out for him.

"Suzie… what are you actually saying?"

She stood up, and thrust the pushchair towards him. "He's three weeks old. Everything you need for him is in his bag."

"Suzie, for fuck's sake!" Panic galvanised Dylan onto his feet, knocking into the pushchair handles. "You're his mother, he needs you. You can't just walk away from him."

She was doing exactly that. She turned her back and set off across the sand.

"Suzie! Jesus, Suzie, stop! I don't have the first fucking clue what to do with a baby."

His former wife paused and turned around, her hands flung out to the sides.

"So learn. Or give him up. I don't really care either way as long as I get on that plane without him."

"You can't mean that," he said, appalled.

Suzie sighed and looked at him flatly. "Donovan loves me, Matthew. He takes care of me. He has money."

Dylan laughed. "Yeah, *my* fucking money."

Suzie shrugged, stony-eyed. "He has money," she said again. "He doesn't want your kid." She glanced back at the baby, just once, but her expression didn't change. "Feed him every few hours. Change his nappy. It's not fucking rocket science."

The baby stirred, opening his eyes and blinking up at Dylan. *He had Billy's eyes.*

"What's his name?"

Suzie paused, almost embarrassed. "He doesn't have one."

Dylan sighed heavily at Suzie's retreating back. "He does now."

She walked away without a backward glance, off towards Justin further up the beach, off back home without her ex-husband's bastard child weighing her down.

Kara drove aimlessly, following the coast road. She couldn't go back to the villa. It was Sophie and Lucien's wedding night. If she went back now, they'd rally round her, enveloping her in hugs, wiping her eyes, plying her with brandy as she spilled the whole sorry tale of how she'd been deceived again. Sophie would comfort her, and Lucien would want to kill Dylan, and their wedding day memories would be forever tarnished. Kara had enough experience of that herself to know that she couldn't and wouldn't inflict it on her best friends.

The traffic around her thickened, and she found herself amongst the brash lights and raucous revellers of San Antonio, otherwise known as party central. She could park up the Mustang and lose herself here amongst these people. Drink until she couldn't remember who she was. Screw someone without even asking his name, and forget the man who hadn't loved her enough to bother even telling her the truth about his own.

People spilled out onto the pavements from the neon-lit bars on either side of the road, laughing, shouting, kissing.

She drove on, leaden-hearted, until the lights thinned out again, and then on some more, meandering around the island until she found herself drawn to somewhere familiar. She swung the Mustang down a sandy lane, nosed through the fringe of pine trees, and turned off the engine as her wheels touched the edge of the sand.

And there she stayed all night, dry-eyed and empty-hearted, overlooking the beach where she'd made love beside a campfire with a make-believe man called Dylan Day.

Chapter Thirty-Eight

One look at Kara's pale face when she walked into the villa at just after seven the following morning was enough to tell Sophie that something was very, very wrong.

Why was she here at all? Sophie frowned, trying to make sense of it amongst the happy detritus of yesterday in her head. Kara was supposed to be with loved up with Dylan. All thoughts of the blissful wedding night she'd just spent with Lucien flew from her mind as she put the coffee cups down with a clatter and half-ran across the room.

"Kara," she cried, taking in her best friend's dishevelled bridesmaid dress and mascara-streaked cheeks. "What happened?" Her mind raced with disastrous scenarios. *Had there been an accident?* "Is Dylan okay?" she pressed. *It had to be Dylan.* Kara's face was ashen as she put down her keys and shook her head.

"No."

Kara's expression was so foreboding that Sophie's hands flew to her cheeks and tears spiked her eyelashes. "What's happened? Tell me, Kara. What is it?"

Kara lifted her tired eyes, realising that Sophie had misunderstood.

"Don't worry Soph," she sighed. "He isn't hurt."

Relief unclouded Sophie's features, followed swiftly by confusion and concern. "So… what is it, then?"

Kara flopped wearily on the sofa and Sophie followed her, tight with anxiety. At that moment, Lucien appeared up the stairs, his hair still mussed from Sophie's fingers, naked aside from his oldest, most loved pair of jeans, T-shirt in hand. The honeymooner smile dropped from his mouth as he looked at their two faces: Sophie's worried and Kara's something far, far worse. In a moment he was hunkered down next to them, his senses on high alert, a feeling of apprehension chilling him and overriding the warmth of the morning.

Sophie rubbed Kara's back, willing her to explain, willing her to be all right.

"What's wrong, honey?"

Kara put her elbows on her knees and dropped her forehead on her palms.

"Just about everything, Soph."

They sat in silence for a few seconds, each of them wrestling with their own questions. Sophie knew that Kara had been planning to declare her love to Dylan. Had he thrown it back in her face? Thinking back to Dylan's expression as he'd danced with Kara at the wedding yesterday, she couldn't make any sense of it if so. He loved her, of that much Sophie was certain.

Lucien sat on Kara's other side, deeply troubled. He knew more about Dylan than either of the women beside him. Had he been complicit in Kara's distress by holding his silence? Could he have prevented this?

"I've been an idiot all over again," Kara said at last, her eyes downcast. "A gullible, stupid fucking idiot." She shook her head and closed her eyes. She was tired - really, really tired - and as Sophie's arm settled around her shoulders and she leaned into her for comfort, her remaining self-possession deserted her.

"Lies, Soph. Lie, after lie, after lie." She batted the tears from her cheeks with the back of her hand, furious with herself for crying over him. "I didn't even know his fucking name."

She knew that she wasn't making a whole lot of sense, and she loved Sophie for listening without asking all of the questions that must be racing through her head at that moment. "I thought I loved him, and I didn't even know his name." It seemed ridiculous, it *sounded* ridiculous.

"And do you know it now?" Lucien asked, low and ultra calm.

"Matthew." A long breath left Kara's body, and she closed her eyes again. "His name is Matthew." She didn't even like saying the word. It seemed so utterly unconnected with the man she thought she knew.

Sophie frowned over her friend's dipped head at Lucien, unsure of what was going on, and even more confused by the fact that Lucien didn't seem all that surprised.

"He isn't who I thought he was," Kara said, to neither of them in particular.

"But why would he do that?" Sophie said. "I don't understand why he'd lie."

"Maybe he had his reasons," Lucien said, careful to keep his tone neutral.

"Oh, he had his reasons," Kara said, and a harsh laugh rattled in her throat. "I met them on the beach last night. His wife, and his child."

"Oh no, Kara," Sophie whispered, realising the extent of the betrayal Kara was trying to process. She squeezed her friend's ramrod-stiff shoulder tighter. This couldn't be happening. Not again. "I'm so sorry, darling."

"Fuck," Lucien said. "Fuck." He scrubbed his hand through his hair and stood up, grabbing his T-shirt from where he'd dropped it and shrugging it over his head. "I'm going down there."

"Lucien, don't." Kara said dully. "There's no point."

Sophie glanced up, knowing from his dark, purposeful expression that Kara's words wouldn't stop him. He grabbed his keys from the stone side table and stalked out of the door.

Betrayal burned hot in Lucien's mind as he drove down the coast. He'd trusted Dylan too. He'd brought the man into their lives and their home, and he'd covered for him when the chips were down. But a wife, and a child? He couldn't fathom how they fitted into the picture that Dylan had drawn for him. Lucien trusted his own instincts, and cheating jarred with everything in his mental assessment of Dylan Day. But it was hardly something that Kara could have been mistaken about. He could almost feel his brain unpicking all of the ties that he'd thought had bound them together as similar men, re-assessing, distancing himself from someone he'd thought he had the measure of.

It wasn't just injured pride at having been taken in. It cut deeper than that. Lucien had lowered his guard because he'd thought they were friends, and his life had felt richer because of it. He thumped his hand down on the steering wheel, furious with Dylan, and also with himself.

He'd let Dylan into their lives, and it was down to him to kick him out again.

Today he was going to lose not only his club manager, but also someone he'd come to think of as a kindred spirit and true friend.

Chapter Thirty-Nine

It had not been an easy night aboard the Love Tug.

Dylan didn't even know how to hold a baby, let alone feed one or change its nappy. Suzie had left him with two drums of formula milk powder, a packet of nappies, four sleep suits, a half used pack of wipes, an open shaker of baby powder… and the baby. Surely the baby needed more than this to stay alive?

Feed him every few hours, she'd said. On what? How much? How often? He had no clue, and his head was all kinds of screwed up. He couldn't think about Kara, because every thought of her hit him like a blow to the stomach and rendered him even more incapable of caring for the tiny human being now sharing the Love Tug. A tiny human being with massive lung capacity, if the amount of screaming he'd done during the night was anything to go by.

Out of frustration, he'd considered emailing his mother at around three am, desperate to know how to make the baby stop the head-splitting noise. But then he'd thought it through, and he'd known she'd put herself on the first flight out, even though she had a pathological fear of flying, and he'd feel like a complete shit when she got here and saw him living on a freak show boat with a wild-haired baby, outcast and jobless to boot. So he'd picked the baby up instead, and one whiff had told him exactly why he was howling like a banshee.

The amount of crap one small baby could produce had been a revelation that Dylan could really have done without in the small hours of the morning, when his life had just crashed down around his ears. As it was, the baby was plastered, all up his back, down his legs… it was a full stripdown situation. Dylan heaved his way through the process of peeling the baby's clothes off and wiping him down, finally resorting to dunking him in the tiny kitchen sink, where he screamed even louder throughout his unceremonious bath.

Was it normal for babies to turn purple when they were mad? He'd finally quieted when Dylan wrapped him in the biggest towel he could find and held him against his shoulder while he tried to mix formula from the instructions on the side of the tin. He'd taken him up on deck and settled into one of the low-slung deckchairs to feed him as the sun came up over the horizon, heralding the start of a brand new day.

His first day as a father, and his first day without Kara. He closed his eyes a few seconds after his son did, equally exhausted and infinitely more terrified.

Chapter Forty

Lucien stalked across the beach at Vadella, still deserted aside from a couple of early dog walkers and a yoga class in session on the sand outside a cafe. He jogged past the impressive boats moored in the bay, all the way to the smallest boat moored at the very end. Although he knew where Dylan was staying, he hadn't visited. And like most visitors, he'd never seen anything like it before. Lucien lifted his sunglasses to peer more closely at the Love Tug as he drew level, then dropped them again hastily, assaulted by the carnival of clashing colours that hit his eyeballs. Trying to put aside his newly formed personal opinion on Dylan's choice of abode, he stepped on board and peered inside through the open sliding door. A can of formula milk sat on the counter, and the kitchen looked and smelled as if a bomb of baby powder had been detonated in there. The presence of a pushchair in the small space confirmed it. There was a baby on board.

"I'm up here."

Dylan's voice came from the roof deck, low and resigned.

Lucien backed out of the junked kitchen and stepped up onto the roof deck. He surveyed the scene in silence. Dylan's tired, haggard face, and the tiny infant swaddled in a towel in his arms.

"Seems the rumours are true then," he said eventually. "Should I say congratulations? Offer you a cigar?" He enjoyed the flare of anguish that his words ignited in Dylan's exhausted eyes. "Where's your wife? Still in bed after your fucking reunion?"

"Ex-wife," Dylan said, monotone. "We aren't married any

more." He looked up at Lucien, the sun's glare hurting his eyes. "Sit down, please man."

"I'll stand."

Dylan shook his head, resigned. He couldn't blame him.

"She's gone, for what it's worth. My ex-wife. She came, dumped a kid on me I didn't know existed, and then she left again with my fuckwit of a brother in tow as her escort."

Lucien stared at him for a long time, and then dropped into the seat opposite Dylan's.

"Spectacular fuck up."

"I know that."

"I should lay you out cold for what you've done to Kara."

"I wouldn't hit you back."

Lucien looked out over the mirror-still water, his mind on the broken girl back at the villa. She was the closest thing he had to a sister.

"That's the thing about Kara. She's bold, and people can mistake that for tough."

"I didn't mistake it."

"No. But you went ahead and hurt her anyway, which is worse," Lucien said. "And the most fucked up thing is that if you'd just had the balls to tell her the whole unvarnished truth, she'd probably have loved you anyway."

Dylan closed his eyes and sighed wearily as he leaned his head back against the wooden back of the chair, but Lucien knew that every word was going in. He went on, relentless, "She has a heart as big as anyone I know, and you've broken it by lying to her."

Dylan scrubbed his hand over his eyes.

"How is she?" he said, so quietly that Lucien almost missed it.

"Do you really need me to fucking answer that?"

Dylan didn't. He knew exactly how hurt Kara was, because he'd hurt himself exactly the same. He wanted Lucien to understand that, but the words wouldn't put themselves together properly in his sleep-deprived mind.

"It seemed so goddamn simple when I came here," he said. "I

just wanted to live an uncomplicated life. Everything back home was fucked up."

"Trouble has a way of following trouble," Lucien said.

Dylan huffed. "Doesn't it just."

The baby stirred against his bare chest, and he fell silent for a second. "I should never have married Suzie. It was a stupid, drunken mistake that we both regretted the morning after. We didn't love each other. Hell, a lot of the time we didn't even like each other." He looked over at Lucien's unreadable face. "She threw her lot in with the wrong crowd, skipped town months ago with the guy who took my club in recompense for Justin's debts." He paused. "I missed the club for a while."

Lucien was listening without comment, and Dylan was grateful. Now he'd started talking, he didn't want to stop till the end. He wanted it all out, now.

"So when I got off the plane here and someone asked me my name, I lied." He shook his head. "Dylan fucking Day. You have no idea how much easier it was to sleep at night." The baby wriggled again, and laid his small, soft palm flat against Dylan's chest, his fingers so tiny they were almost translucent. "And however crazy and fucked up it sounds, in here," Dylan touched his fingers against his heart, "In here, I *feel* like Dylan Day. I didn't lie to hide the truth. I lied because I couldn't stand to be Matthew McKenzie any longer. The world I grew up in wasn't like this, Lucien."

Lucien knew more than Dylan could possibly realise about inventing a different life for yourself because the one you have sucks.

"I don't expect you to understand, and I'm not asking for your sympathy." Dylan went on. "If I could wind the clock back and change things I would, but life doesn't work like that, does it?" He levered himself up to sit straighter as the baby opened his eyes. Both men looked down at the child as he roused. "And then there's him. A boy with a fraud for a father and a mother who doesn't want him."

Lucien frowned. "She's left him with you for good?"

Dylan nodded. " And I don't have the first fucking clue what to do with a baby." He moved the child awkwardly in his arms and the towel fell open. On cue, an arc of pee spouted all over Dylan's knee, and both men looked on, aghast.

"Jesus, man. He needs a nappy."

"I tried, they kept falling off," Dylan said, exasperated. He mopped his leg with the corner of the towel as the baby fastened his gums around the bent thumb of his other hand. "Jesus. No one told me babies bite," he said, trying to extricate his hand gently.

"I think he's trying to tell you that he's hungry," Lucien said, and sighed with resignation. "Where are the nappies?"

Half an hour and a master class in the art of nappy changing later, Lucien picked up the baby boy and sat him on his knee, cradling his head in the way only a practised father can. He contemplated the tiny child for a moment and then looked up at Dylan.

"He has ridiculous hair."

Dylan smiled for the first time since the moment he'd laid eyes on Justin last night. A half smile, a tired smile, but a smile, of sorts. "I kinda like it."

Lucien nodded, digesting the implications of the comment. "I take it you're planning to keep him?"

Dylan nodded. There was no question in his mind. From the moment that the baby had opened his eyes and looked at him last night, he'd known what he had to do.

"He's my son. My responsibility."

"And you're going to live where? Here? On this boat with a baby?"

"Lucien, I don't have a fucking clue what happens next. I didn't know he existed this time yesterday. I'm not even sure how to keep him alive, but one way or another, yes. He stays with me."

Lucien had to respect the conviction with which Dylan had

accepted the parental responsibilities so unpromisingly foisted on him.

He scrubbed his hand over his chin, at war with himself, because the truth was that sitting there listening to Dylan, he almost understood.

He couldn't condone the fact that he'd lied, but he *could* understand how one lie had led to the next, and that none of those lies had been borne of maliciousness or an underhand attempt to deceive.

But then he thought of Kara, hollow-eyed and heartbroken, and he wanted to grab Dylan around the throat out of pure frustration.

"And what about Kara?" he said.

"Kara." Dylan said her name with the quiet reverence of a priest, then closed his eyes and sighed raggedly. Lucien looked away, settling the baby in the crook of his arm to give Dylan a few seconds to get himself back together.

"I've never met anyone like Kara before," Dylan said. "She is good, and clean, and pure, and all of the things I'm not. She was falling for Dylan Day, and she made me want to be him forever. I still do. I can't go back to life as Matthew McKenzie." He looked down at the baby. "Especially not now."

Lucien didn't envy Dylan his new life as a single father. It seemed unfathomable that they were even having this discussion, when just yesterday they'd all laughed and toasted their idyllic Ibizan summer.

"Tell her I'm sorry?"

"You know I can't do that."

Dylan nodded. "These past few months have been the best of my life."

Lucien looked down at Dylan's son. "That's good. Because these next few will be amongst the hardest."

Chapter Forty-One

Lucien found Sophie sitting alone at the dining table when he returned to the villa a little while later. She looked up immediately as he came in the door, her face a study of concern as he dropped into the seat opposite her.

"Did you see him?"

He glanced over his shoulder. "Where's Kara?"

Sophie shook her head miserably. "She's gone."

"Gone? Gone where?"

"Home. Back to England. She threw her things into a bag just after you left. I couldn't persuade her to stay. I couldn't even get her to let me take her to the airport."

Lucien pushed his hands through his hair. He'd been gone a few hours. Numerous flights left the airport every day bound for the UK: there was every chance that Kara was already airborne.

"What an absolute fucking mess."

"She couldn't stand the idea of running into Dylan again. She was desperate." Tears filled Sophie's eyes. "I'm so worried about her Lucien. She went through so much with Richard, I really thought Dylan was…" her words tailed off as a tear dripped from her cheek into the mug of cold coffee cradled in her hands.

"I know, Princess," Lucien said. "I know."

"So did you see him?" she asked again, and this time Lucien nodded.

"Yes. I saw him."

Sophie's head snapped up, her eyes blazing.

"What did he have to say for himself?"

"It's complicated, Soph," Lucien said softly after a couple of seconds, making her frown.

"Please don't tell me you're about to defend him," she said quietly.

Lucien sighed. "I'm not defending him. It's just not as cut and dried as you think."

She stared at him blankly. "If he has a wife and child, then it's pretty cut and dried from where I'm standing."

"She's his ex-wife. They *are* divorced."

"But she still turned up here, and he has a child with her. Was she there?"

Lucien shook his head. "No. She's gone."

Sophie looked at him steadily, waiting for more.

"She's gone, Sophie. She dumped a three week old kid on Dylan and then shot through back to the rock she crawled from under."

It was too ridiculous an idea for Sophie to process. "*She left a three week old baby?* For how long?"

Lucien nodded. "Forever. He's all kinds of screwed."

Sophie took the news in.

"Do you expect me to feel sorry for him?" she asked after a moment. "Because I don't. For the baby maybe, but not for him."

"I get that."

Sophie shook her head, not convinced Lucien did get it. He'd left the house furious and returned almost ready to fight Dylan's corner. Dylan, or *Matthew*, or whoever he was, was clearly a very accomplished liar, because Lucien didn't suffer fools gladly.

Still she couldn't find it within herself to be mad at Lucien for wavering. She'd watched him grow close to Dylan over the months, and it had warmed her to see those bonds of friendship.

Over their years together she'd watched him learn to open his heart, first of all to her, and then to Tilly, and over time he'd encompassed Kara in his circle of trust. Dylan had brought something new and unfamiliar to his life, a sense of brotherhood and friendship that he'd never before known as a grown man. It wounded her to think he was going to lose that, and it wounded her to think that Dylan wasn't the man she'd honestly believed him to be.

She'd thought him a better man. A man worthy of Lucien's trust, a man worthy of Kara's love.

"I need to go home too," she said gently. "I need to go back for Kara. The staff at the boutique are ready anyway, it'll just mean bringing the handover forward a couple of weeks." She'd already spoken briefly with Aida, their assistant manager, after Kara had left, and set the wheels in motion for her own early departure. Their flights were arranged, and Esther was packing Tilly's things up as they spoke. She knew Kara well enough to know that she wouldn't go running to her family and friends for support when she arrived back in England. She'd try to shoulder her burden alone, most likely drowning her sorrows in the bottom of countless wine bottles. Sophie had been there herself, and she shuddered to think what might have become of her if Kara hadn't come to her rescue with her unique blend of common sense, good humour and tough love.

"I'll have to stay on here, for a couple of weeks at least," Lucien said, disgruntled but resigned. He accepted immediately that Sophie needed to be there for her friend. For *their* friend. "There's no way Dylan's in any position to come into work."

"Do we still even call him Dylan?"

Lucien studied her face. "He's still the same man, Sophie," he said, and the despondent expression in his eyes sliced through her heart. "Sometimes good people do bad things for good reasons."

She stared at him for a long time. "And do you think he had good reason?"

Lucien shrugged. "The jury's out. Go home and take care of Kara. She's the one who matters right now."

Chapter Forty-Two

As it turned out, Kara hadn't sought comfort in the bottom of a wine bottle. Not because she didn't want a drink, but because she wanted one so much she feared that she'd drown her own lungs in alcohol if she let herself pour so much as a glass. She had previous form in heartache, after all, or somewhere on the scale, at least. When Richard had jilted her at the altar, she'd anaesthetised the pain and humiliation with liquor. She knew now that it didn't really help. She'd thought at the time that she couldn't possibly feel worse. She also knew now that she'd been very, very wrong.

Loving and losing Dylan Day made what Richard had put her through seem like a walk in the park.

The transition from loved to lonely had all happened so fast. Two weeks on and she was still reeling from the impact of that night on the beach, nurturing a glowing ball of pure hatred for the man who'd melted her heart and then stamped all over it.

He'd been so very, very lovely. How could it not have been real? Never for one second had she harboured even the tiniest of doubts, yet their entire time together had been nothing more than a fabrication.

Her emotions veered wildly between the raw, gaping misery of loss and fury hot enough to want him dead. How dare he? How fucking dare he? She'd lost any faith in her own ability to know the bottom from the top, he'd robbed her of her self respect and dignity right along with her heart. Twice already she'd looked up flight information to Ibiza, half certain that she wanted to go back and face him, to make him tell her what she'd done to deserve it. Had he been looking for someone to lay the con on and judged her gullible enough to be the one? Someone to warm his bed in the absence of his wife? But why go to all that trouble? He could have found any number of willing women on Ibiza without needing to woo or lie. He was the beautiful boss of a sex club - if anyone could get sex without trying, it was surely him.

Was it just the thrill of the chase that turned him on? Or did he get his kicks from lying, from watching her fall into his web of deceit?

All of these thoughts and many other, darker ones filled Kara's brain on a loop until she held her head in her hands and cried, needing the haranguing voices to stop.

He was married. He was divorced. He had a child. The child wasn't his. The child was his. He'd lied about so many things that she had no clue which amongst them were the truth anymore.

She didn't get up from the kitchen table when she heard Sophie's key in the door, but she was relieved to hear it none the less, grateful always for her friend's quiet, strong solidarity at her side.

Sophie came into the room, flicking the kettle on as she passed it, toting carrier bags from which she began to unpack fresh food. She unravelled the soft woollen scarf from her throat and wound it instead around Kara's neck, ruffling her friend's hair. She swiped the cold cup of coffee from Kara's hands and replaced it with a fresh one for each of them.

"Did you sleep last night?"

Kara lifted one shoulder. "Some, I think." She sipped the hot drink and sighed, pulling the folder on the table towards her and flipping it open.

"Remember we talked about the possibility of opening some stand alone boutiques over the next couple of years? I've been doing some research and I think it's got potential." She sifted through the paperwork quickly, frowning. "I made some lists..."

Sophie reached out and stilled Kara's increasingly erratic hands. "Kara, stop."

"No, it's here somewhere. I made lists... locations..."

Sophie squeezed her fingers, knowing full well that Kara was using work to block out thoughts of Dylan. "Okay," she said. "We'll find the list, and we can talk about work if you want to, but you can't pretend that this hasn't happened forever, you know?"

Kara withdrew her hands and propped her forehead in them instead.

"It's all I've got right now, Soph." She sighed heavily. It wasn't all she wanted, but it was all she'd got. Every time Sophie came she battled with herself not to ask questions about Dylan. Today, she lost her battle.

"Have you spoken to Lucien today?"

Sophie nodded. They spoke all the time. She stroked her wedding ring beneath the table top, wishing he was here instead of still wrapping things up on Ibiza. A one-night honeymoon wasn't what they'd had in mind.

"And is *he* still there?" Kara asked tonelessly, and Sophie didn't need to wonder who she meant. She faltered, wondering how her friend was going to take the news.

"For now. He told Lucien yesterday that he's decided it's time to move on."

Kara let the information sink in. "Move on where?"

"He didn't say. Back to the States, I expect?"

The man Kara had thought she knew wouldn't head back to the States. A slow, cold creep of panic stole over her bones.

He was going to disappear, and she'd never see him again.

But so what, she hated him.

He was going to disappear, and she'd never get the chance to force him to answer all of the questions that haunted her.

But he wasn't worth even one single moment more of her time.

He was going to disappear, and she'd never have the chance to beat her fists on his chest until he was as black and blue on the outside as she was on the inside.

But he didn't deserve to feel the touch of her hand ever again, even in anger.

He was going to disappear.

Dylan needed to disappear. It had been two weeks since Kara had left, two weeks since Billy had arrived.

It seemed a lifetime longer on both counts. He needed to step up to the plate and make a plan for the future, find some place to lay down roots for Billy, a job with regular hours.

The baby had turned his entire world upside down and inside out. He wasn't just a tiny person. He was a mini-dictator, and Dylan his foot soldier as much as his father. The first few days had been a living hell of not knowing why Billy was screaming or how to make it stop, but little by little, he was learning to read his son's cues. He wasn't confident that he was doing a very good job, but he did at least feel pretty sure that he could keep Billy alive and well, which was several significant steps forward from the day Suzie had left him literally holding the baby.

He owed most of his new knowledge and a big debt of gratitude to Lucien. He'd fully expected to find himself unemployed and unwelcome, but Lucien had turned out to be a measured, loyal friend who didn't turn away in times of trouble. Dylan knew that Lucien had found himself caught in the most delicate of positions, and his admiration for the other man deepened ten-fold as he observed how he managed to remain true to himself without feeling obligated to entrench himself on one side or the other.

Instead of firing him, he'd given him paternity leave. *Paid* paternity leave. Company rules, he'd said.

No big deal, he'd said.

But it *was* a big deal. A big, huge deal. It was the gift of precious breathing space, of time to get a handle on the enormity of what had happened to him, to get to know his baby, to grieve for the love he'd lost.

Billy was the most effective distraction imaginable when he was awake, but when he slept, Kara came. She came to Dylan in his daydreams and in the snatches of sleep he managed at night, sometimes smiling, sometimes furious, and beautiful all the time. His whole body ached with missing her, as if he'd been trampled by wild horses.

The only time of day when he could find any solace at all came at sunset. Most nights, Billy's fledgling routine allowed for him to be fed, winded and bathed by then, and they'd developed a habit of sitting up on deck, one man and his baby, to watch the horizon darken.

Billy seemed able to sleep easiest held skin to skin, his tiny chest against his daddy's, his blanket tucked around him until just his small round face and wild-child hair poked out above. Dylan often found his own eyes closing too, drifting into a doze along with his son.

It was there, in that exact position, that Kara found him, two weeks and two days almost to the hour after she'd left.

Chapter Forty-Three

It was the way he cradled the damn baby that made her cry. All of that big, powerful strength rendered gentle and tender by the presence of the infant in his arms. How could a man who held a baby with such infinite care be the same man who'd broken her heart?

Kara wiped her fingertips over her damp cheeks, glad that Dylan was sleeping. He didn't deserve to see her tears.

She wavered, uncertain, considered walking away. She'd come here in anger, with an outraged sense of unfinished business, fury that he'd left her feeling a million times worse than Richard had. If she let it go by the wayside without ever setting the record straight, she feared that she'd never trust her own instincts again. Her self respect was a cause worth fighting for. But now he was here in front of her, she realised she'd come for something else too. She'd come to be near him one last time: her traitorous heart hadn't yet completely cast him out and the knowledge of this scared her witless. *If he opened his eyes now and lied some more, would she believe him?* Her faith in herself was on the floor because of Dylan Day.

Then he opened his eyes.

"English." He spoke on the softest of intakes of breath as he looked at her, and the expression in his eyes confirmed Kara's fears. She was in trouble, because she could see him going through the same overwhelming emotions that she'd experienced herself a few minutes earlier. She saw it all play out on his face: incredulous surprise, the bright, against-all-odds flare of hope, and then the bitter, crushing weight of disappointment.

Kara didn't speak because she found herself out of suitable words.

He glanced down at the sleeping baby, and then back up at her.

"I'll go and put him in bed," he said, getting up carefully. He turned back before he disappeared inside, uncertainty on his face. "I'll be a couple of minutes…please don't go."

And there it was again, that hot ball of tears burning her throat. She didn't answer him, just turned away and sat down in the low deck chair he'd vacated. The heat from his body warmed hers.

Yes. She'd wait.

Below deck, Dylan laid the baby down in the makeshift cradle he'd fashioned himself over the last couple of days. He could have bought one, but the idea of a shopping trip with a baby in tow terrified him, and besides, he'd needed to keep his mind busy during Billy's naptimes. It'd never grace the pages of a design magazine, but it was good enough, and that needed to *be* enough, for now at least.

Kara was here. He'd worked hard on resigning himself to the fact that he'd never see her again, but she was actually here, right now, here on his deck, cowboy boots and all, and he had no idea how the hell to play it.

He unfolded a second chair on deck a few minutes later and sat down alongside her. The answer was simple. He would play it straight. He owed her that at the very least.

"Why are you here, Kara?"

His question held no trace of confrontation, more a resigned sense of defeat.

"To hear the truth from you, I guess." Kara shook her head, her eyes on the horizon. "I need to know why. Was it all a big game for you?"

"Kara, no…"

"I wake up every day and wonder how I could have been such a monumental fool. I thought I knew better, but it feels like I'm the girl who never learns her lessons. My father. Richard. You. Is there something about me that marks me out as a pushover, Dylan? Something pathetic, needy?"

Deep frown lines creased his brow.

"I lied, Kara. I lied and you believed me, which makes you a good, trusting person, which is a fucking miracle given the number of people who've let you down. That I'm the latest name on that damn list kills me."

"I hear you're planning to disappear," she said tonelessly. She'd come here to reclaim her self-respect, even if it meant stripping him of his. "That makes you a man who lies and then runs from his problems. Not exactly daddy of the year material. I should know, I grew up with a father like that, remember?" Anger made her harsh, and she twisted to look him directly in the eyes. "I don't envy your child."

It was a lie. She did. She envied the baby that he'd get to spend every day with Dylan.

But every one of her words hit their target, and he took her arrows because she had every right in the world to hate him.

"Can I tell you the truth?" he asked.

"Oh, that's funny, coming from you," she said. "You mean the sob story about your evil ex-wife dumping your newborn baby on you? Don't bother, I've had it all relayed second hand already."

Dylan nodded. "I figured you would have heard."

"So what else is there I need to know?"

He sighed heavily, his head leaned against the wooden sidebar of the seat as he looked at her. "I've apologised to you a million times over in my head, Kara. For not finding the right time to tell you all my fucked up, ugly truths, for not giving you the choice to walk away from me, for the fact that you had to find out in such a cruel, humiliating way."

"You should have told me yourself," she said quietly. "I'd have believed anything you told me."

"Maybe. Maybe not. It's not a pretty life back home, Kara."

"You think I'm that shallow?" she said. "I'd rather have ugly truths than pretty lies."

He nodded. "That's the thing, Kara. The lies weren't for your benefit. They were for mine. It was a fairytale. *My* fairytale. One where my brother hadn't died, where I hadn't married a woman I didn't love, one where I didn't lose everything I ever owned." The fierce longing in his eyes held hers. "I needed a holiday from my real life, but I didn't count on you. You were so much more than a holiday romance. You made me want to be Dylan Day forever."

"I wanted you to be him too," she whispered, her tears threatening again. She'd loved him so very, very much.

He looked at her, brittle and broken, and he knew that the moment had arrived, finally, to do the right thing by the woman he loved.

"Kara, I miss you every day. Every morning. Every night. All of the time." He badly needed her to know how very much she meant to him.

"I know it doesn't matter now, and I know you can't come back to me, because it isn't just me any more. It's me and Billy. Billy and me. " The river deep conviction in his voice made her envious of the baby for the second time that evening. "I'm a father, Kara. I have a son. I've been all kinds of stupid, but you're wrong about one thing. I'm not going to be a bad father to Billy. Maybe I suck at it right now, but I'm learning. He stops crying when I hold him, so I figure I must be doing something right. And I'll get better. I won't lie to him, or let him down. I'll do the best I can and hope like hell that it's enough."

It was the speech of his lifetime, the protective words of a new father who loved his child, and for a few seconds they stared at each other, shell-shocked. She made his heart ache. He made her heart break.

"Go home Kara. Go home and be happy, because you deserve to be more than anyone else I know. Go home knowing that I truly fucking loved you. You didn't get it wrong. I didn't fool you, and the next man who loves you won't automatically be lying to you. He'll be the luckiest guy in the world. Don't run away from love because of what I did. I lied about many things, but never once about how I felt about you."

Kara stopped trying to hold her tears in. It was a battle she'd never win, and Dylan was barely hanging on himself. He reached out and brushed the back of his fingers over her damp cheek.

"Go home knowing I love your huge fucking heart, and your laugh, and the way you do everything full throttle even though there's every chance you'll break your neck. I'm not going to ask you to stay. Not because I don't want you, or because I don't love you, or because I don't need you. I do. I love you, and I want you, and I need you so much it hurts to wake up in the morning without you." His voice cracked. "Let that be my liar's penance."

He stood up, and she took the hand he held out and stood up with him beneath the Ibizan stars, back on the deck where it had all begun. He settled his jacket around her cool shoulders, then pulled her close and kissed the top of her head for a long time. When he stepped back and held both of her hands tight in his, Kara never wanted him to let go.

"You are the fucking coolest girl I've ever met, and the craziest, and the kindest," he said softly. "Go home, English. You're out of my league. You always were."

She left him standing there, knowing he was right, wishing he was wrong. She couldn't stay. Everything had changed, yet he'd given her so much more than she'd come for. He'd restored her self-respect, and he'd set her back on her feet as a woman. So why didn't she feel whole again?

The thing he hadn't given her back was her heart. Dylan Day was a man who was going to take a lot of getting over.

Chapter Forty-Four

Kara sat at a small, scrubbed pine table inside the Happy Days Beach Bar nursing her second cup of coffee of the morning, her eyes scanning the sand. The summer crowds had left the island now, leaving the beaches to a different clientele who took Ibizan life at a gentler pace. It was still early as she watched the sunbeds being laid out in ranks across the sands, their padded cream cushions a touch of luxury for the well-heeled off-season crowd.

She couldn't see the Love Tug from her vantage point, but that was okay. She wasn't in any hurry.

Dylan strapped Billy to his chest in the cotton baby-carrier that one of the boutique staff from the club had donated to him, along with a box of sleep suits and baby clothes. He'd been astounded by the power of the baby to melt hearts at twenty paces: one look at that shock of hair and big brown eyes and he had them in the palm of his little hand. Dylan hoped for Billy's sake that his power over the opposite sex never dwindled.

"Come on, small guy. Daddy's hungry."

He made his way around the rocky path towards the beach, his path set for the bakery at the far end, his mind set on Kara.

Where was she this morning? Had she gone back to the villa? Lucien was due to go home to England over the next day or two, he'd have been around for her last night. The thought gladdened him. If there was any man he trusted to look out for Kara, that man was Lucien Knight.

Kara tensed as Dylan appeared on the beach. Her breath caught in her throat as she watched him walk by the cafe, barefoot and bare-chested aside from the baby carrier. Even from a distance she could see the baby's startling shock of hair, and a smile touched her lips.

Dylan walked the beach with the ease of a local, pausing briefly to pass the time of day with the guy who dragged the sunbeds across the sands.

She saw him smile, and wanted his smile to be for her. She didn't get up. Just watched him, sure of where he was heading.

She caught the eye of the waitress cleaning a nearby table and ordered another coffee, this time to take away.

Dylan walked slowly back along the beach, the warm, scented pastries in a brown paper bag in his hand. He'd visited the bakery as much out of habit as out of hunger; the familiarity of routine had become important in these most unsettling of days.

He chatted inanely to Billy as he walked back towards the boat, even though the baby couldn't understand a word he said and was half way towards his morning snooze. He didn't even notice that someone was walking towards him until she fell into step beside him on the sand.

"Hey, Sailor," she said softly. "You forgot your jacket."

"You're supposed to be someplace else," he said, gladdened beyond belief that she wasn't. "Anywhere but here with me."

"I have coffee?" she said, knowing that there was nowhere else in the world she'd rather be.

He held the bag up. "And I have pastries."

She moved towards a sun-bed set beneath a thatched umbrella close to the azure shoreline and sat down. Dylan sat alongside her, Billy fast asleep on his chest. Kara looked down at him for a few long, silent seconds.

"That's some hairstyle."

"I know. I kind of like it."

"Me too." She reached out and touched a soft strand of it. "He has a good name."

"The best," Dylan said without missing a beat.

She nodded. "Can I still call you Dylan?"

He stroked the baby's hair and sighed.

"It's just a name, Kara. I'm still the same man, and for what it's worth, I was more myself with you than I've ever been with anyone else."

She reached for the pastry bag he'd placed down on the sunbed between them and ripped it open.

"I know that now." She passed him the coffee, and then teased a warm pastry apart in her fingers. "I couldn't get on the plane back to England. I tried, I really did. I queued, but when it came to my turn, I couldn't get on the damn plane."

He sipped the scalding drink from the tiny hole in the lid, leaning sideways so as not to hold it over Billy's head.

"You should have."

"Should I?"

Dylan placed the cup down and accepted the chunk of pastry she held out.

"It would have been the sensible choice."

"I don't do sensible. I do full throttle, even though it might break my neck," she said. "Or my heart."

"I never wanted to break your heart, English."

"You put it back together again last night."

"I broke my own heart too, if it's any consolation."

They sat in silence then, man, woman and child.

She screwed up the empty pastry bag, set the coffee cup down in the sand, and sank back against the sun lounger. "Lie with me for a while?"

Dylan swallowed hard. He wanted to lie there with Kara so much that he feared his banging heart might wake Billy. He lay back slowly beside her and offered her the crook of his shoulder. She met his eyes for an uncertain second and then accepted, settling herself against the warmth of his body.

He was so warm. So warm, and vital, and so intrinsically,

basically right that she sighed heavily. His arms felt like her home.

"Dylan…" she said.

He stroked her hair. "Ssh. Just for one minute. Don't say anything."

And so she didn't. She closed her eyes and let him stroke her hair, her arm flung across his midriff beneath Billy's tiny toes.

Little by little she tilted her face, and little by little he dipped his, until his mouth was a breath away from her own.

He opened his eyes, and in hers he found absolution.

She opened her eyes, and in his she found devotion.

"How are we gonna play this thing, English?" he said, cupping her face with his palm.

"One day at a time," she whispered. "Kiss me?"

His gaze fell to her lips, and then back up to her eyes. No kiss had ever felt so important.

Her gentle sigh of longing filled his head when he lowered his mouth over hers. "Kara," he whispered, her name his prayer as he closed his eyes and let his feelings take over. Her mouth opened and invited him in, let his tongue slide over hers, into her heart, her everything. He buried his hand in her hair and held her head to his. "I love you so very much," he breathed, and then he kissed her again, aching all over with how much she meant to him.

She hadn't said why she was here, or if she intended to stay, but he needed to say it anyway, and he needed her to hear it.

"I love you too," she said, her hand gentle over the warm skin at the nape of his neck when he lifted his head. "Can I stay?"

Dylan eased back, his fingers still on her jaw. Such a casually phrased question, but he could feel her trembling.

"Are you sure you want to?"

Kara looked at him, clear eyed and very, very clear in her mind.

"I'll never love anyone else the way I love you. I've never been more sure of anything in my life."

"It's not just me, Kara," he said, glancing down at the top of Billy's head. "We're kind of a package deal."

"Hey, the cute baby clinched it," she smiled, stroking the baby's foot. "You should thank him someday."

"Every day for the rest of my life."

"I'm going to stick around to make sure you do, Sailor."

Dylan kissed her hair as she settled her head on his shoulder and looked out towards the sea, towards the Love Tug nestled at the far end of the rocks.

"I knew the moment I saw that crazy-ass boat that I was in trouble," she said.

"But you didn't turn around and walk away."

"Trouble is my middle name."

"Then we match." Kara felt his soft laugh against her hair.

"I don't know the first thing about babies. Just so you know," she said, and touched Billy's pink cheek.

"Me neither, but I'm learning," Dylan said. He reached down and un-clipped the baby carrier carefully, then manoeuvred the still sleeping Billy down onto the cushion of the shaded lounger. Unencumbered now, he stood, and Kara stood with him.

"Come here, English," he said gently, pulling her near. She wrapped her arms around him and closed her eyes, breathing his scent in deep as his restless hands moved over her back, in her hair, over the flare of her hips.

"You fit me, Kara," he said. "You know every fucked up part of me, and you still see someone you can love."

She wrapped him closer. So much man. So much more than he gave himself credit for. "You fit me, Sailor." She tipped her head back and offered him her mouth, an offer he accepted and then some, kissing her breath away. They lingered at the water's edge, eyes closed, her face in his hands as his tongue moved against hers. Love and lust sparkled low in her stomach, as warm and welcome as a summer's day.

"You feel that?" he said, his voice raw with emotion.

"I feel it." She didn't have the words to tell him how much.

"Say you'll never go," he said, even though he'd promised himself he wouldn't ask it of her.

"Tell me you want me to stay forever," she murmured, knowing he was the love of her lifetime.

"Always, English," he said. "Always."

Epilogue

Ibiza, two years later.

"Not much further now," Kara laughed, tugging Dylan along the beach. He almost stumbled on a rock in the sand and reached up to push off the blindfold Kara had insisted he wear for the duration of the car journey from the villa. She'd been elated and giddy all day, a sure indication that she was up to no good.

"No, don't," she said, catching his arm and smacking it away. "You'll spoil the surprise."

"I've told you what I want for my birthday," he grumbled.

"And you'll get me." She stroked her hand down his ass, enjoying him being at her mercy. "Later. After your surprise."

She tugged him towards the rocks at the end of the beach and then stopped and slid her arms around him.

"This surprise just got a whole lot more interesting," he murmured, running his hands down her spine appreciatively through her clinging dress. He kissed her, hot and open mouthed, his hands moving over her body, and for a little while all thoughts of the surprise waiting at the end of the rocks flew out of her head.

"This isn't the first time you've blindfolded me on my birthday," he murmured, and she laughed softly into his kiss, remembering.

"I know." She slid her hands beneath his T-shirt. "You trusted me then."

"I trust you now. Untie the blindfold, English," he said, his hand cupping her cheek. "I want to look at you."

She kissed him once more, long and lingering as she slowly untied the blindfold, letting her hands play in his hair as she took her time over loosening the fastening. Finally he blinked around, freed, letting his eyes adjust to the starlit night.

Recognition flitted across his face as he took in his surroundings. "Vadella," he said simply, with a smile.

Kara nodded and took his hand. He narrowed his eyes as she smiled serenely and led him along the rocky path at the edge of the beach. He hadn't walked the path in a good while, not since it became apparent very soon after Billy's arrival that babies and boats didn't mix. Not boats like the one he'd called home, in any case. The pretty hillside villa he shared now with Kara and his toddler son afforded them more space and convenience and presented many fewer hazards for a wobbly new walker and inquisitive explorer, though it had to be said, it lacked the kitsch charm of Dylan's previous abode. Very occasionally, he missed the old boat's quirks.

They passed by the newer boats moored there now, including several impressive looking cruisers and a couple of fishing boats, and Kara kept going all the way along to the very end of the rocks. So they were going back.

Back to the Love Tug.

Dylan started to laugh softly. He could see it lit up ahead now, the multi-coloured fairy lights around the railings of the deck winking bright against the dark skies, low music floating out from the speakers.

"Have dinner with me?" Kara said, and the look in her eyes promised a whole lot more besides.

"You know all the best places to eat," he said. "Let me guess. Take-out paella?"

"Not exactly," she said with a small, uncharacteristically nervous smile. She handed him a set of keys he recognised instantly.

"It's yours," she said, watching his face as her words sank in. *"You bought the boat?"*

His incredulous grin wiped the anxiety from her face.

"Every sailor needs a boat," she said, leaning in to kiss him. "Or a weekend shag palace…"

"Shag palace?" he said, mimicking her accent, smiling against her lips. "So English, as always."

Kara loved the sight of him stepping aboard the old boat again. So many good memories were wrapped up in one small, crazy old vessel. She accepted the hand he held out and stepped aboard, the heels of her cowboy boots loud against the deck.

Dylan pulled her against him, running his fingertip along the neckline of the tube dress he loved her in.

"Did you wear this for me?" he said.

"It *is* your birthday." She leaned in close and kissed the warm skin beside his ear. "And I'm not wearing anything underneath it."

"You know I'm going to check that later, right?"

"I'm counting on it, Sailor." She started up the steps to the roof deck, then glanced back over her shoulder at him. "You can look up my skirt. Birthday treat."

Dylan's eyes were so firmly fixed on Kara's backside that it took him a few seconds to realise that they wouldn't be dining alone. Lucien and Sophie sat alongside each other on the familiar low deck chairs, conspirators in Kara's birthday plan. Sophie jumped up as soon as Dylan appeared.

"Happy birthday!" she said, laughing as she threw her arms around him. He hugged her hard, blown away by their surprise arrival on the island. He kissed her cheek when she stepped back.

"You guys have been plotting," Dylan smiled wide and easy. "When did you get here?"

"A few hours ago." Sophie grinned, her eyes dancing with the thrill of the successful ambush. "We dropped Esther and the kids off at yours as soon as you guys went out."

Lucien unfurled himself from the chair as Kara bent to kiss his cheek then pulled Sophie into an expansive hug and led her away below deck.

Lucien advanced towards Dylan.

"Happy Birthday, bud," he said, pressing a bottle of Dylan's favourite bourbon into his hands.

Dylan laughed, still a little shell-shocked by the unexpected birthday gathering.

"It's so good to see you, man," he said, pulling Lucien into a bear hug even though he knew his friend wasn't the most tactile of men. "Drink?" he asked, reaching out of habit into a low cupboard to the side of the deck where barware had always been stored in his time. He found a couple of glass tumblers and uncapped the bottle, splashing amber liquid into them.

They stood alongside each other, elbows on the railings and a generous measure of bourbon in their glasses.

"How long are you guys staying?"

"A week or so," Lucien said. "If you can stand it. Oskar's cutting teeth. We make bad house guests. Trust me, you'll be ready for us to leave."

Dylan grimaced. "Teething, man. Gruesome. Billy screamed for weeks."

They contemplated the sea in silence for a few seconds, both men ruminating on how much had changed since they met.

Lucien and Sophie's family had expanded with the arrival of their son, Oskar, making Tilly a proud and mostly delighted big sister and Lucien an even prouder and more delighted father.

Knight Inc. continued to go from strength to strength, with Lucien on the final countdown to the opening of his eleventh club. The Knight family skipped happily around the globe in his private jet, a tightly knit clan rarely separated for more than a few days.

Kara and Dylan had taken a far more Bohemian approach, and

it worked just fine for their relationship. Living together, absorbing Billy into their routine, his long afternoon siestas affording them the opportunity to make the most of each other's company in all the ways they liked best. Ibiza suited them, and they suited Ibiza, having entrenched themselves firmly amongst the eclectic group of native and part-time residents they now counted as friends.

The Ibizan club had met and then exceeded even Lucien's expectations under Dylan's expert stewardship, so much so that the venture had expanded this season to launch a luxury weekend party boat, currently the hottest ticket in town in every sense of the word. Kara had flexed her business muscles that summer too, opening a standalone boutique on the neighbouring island of Mallorca.

Kara's and Sophie's friendship was stronger and brighter than ever, and their two families grew ever closer, outside of work. They met up as often as their busy schedules would allow; snatched weekends in London, the occasional week soaking up the sun in Ibiza, idyllic Christmastimes in Norway.

It was a good life.

Lucien reached into the battered leather jacket he'd hooked over a chairback, then produced two cigars from the inside pocket. He shrugged, then smiled at Dylan's surprised look. "It's your birthday," he said by way of explanation, coming back to lean beside his friend with a lighter in his hand.

"I haven't had one of these in years." Dylan placed the cigar between his lips, then leaned towards the flame that Lucien sparked. Lucien lit his own cigar and blew out a slow stream of smoke.

"My brother was the cigar smoker of the family," Dylan said, remembering late nights and good times.

Lucien knew from the past tense that Dylan was referring to Billy. He took a deep slug of bourbon, the rich shot of alcohol combining with the taste of the cigar in his mouth. "I never had a brother."

Dylan huffed lightly. "Yeah, well. Take it from me. It's not all good news."

Lucien nodded. From what he'd seen of Dylan's surviving brother, there wasn't anything to envy.

In the moments of companionable silence that followed, nostalgic memories of Billy merged with the closeness Dylan felt to the man beside him now.

"I know this kind of talk makes you freak out, but I'm gonna say it anyway," Dylan said, laughing softly. "I fuckin' love you, man."

"Jesus Christ," Lucien muttered, re-lighting his cigar and holding the flame out to Dylan.

It wasn't his style to make such expansive comments, but he knew what Dylan meant all the same. Theirs was a friendship that he'd come to value very much in the years since their first encounter. Back then, he'd entrusted Dylan with the responsibility of running his club. These days, their bond ran so much deeper; as close as brothers, the best of friends.

He met Dylan's eye in a moment of silent acknowledgement, then shuddered despite the warmth of the evening. "And now I feel like we just had sex." He knocked his bourbon back in one huge slug, and Dylan turned away to hide his smile.

It was the best of evenings.

A million stars lit the sky above them like an incandescent celestial map. Sophie rested her head back on Lucien's arm and looked up as one streaked bright and brilliant across the skies over their heads.

"Shooting star," she said. "Make a wish."

"Can it involve fucking?" Lucien wasn't at all bothered by the fact that they weren't alone. Dylan and Kara knew exactly how it was between them.

Sophie laughed, equally unabashed. "You're getting predictable."

Lucien shook his head. "I don't need to make a wish, Princess," he said, his hand warm on the back of her hair. He glanced around the table. At Dylan and Kara, wrapped up in each other, and then back at Sophie, caught up in him. He loved them all. "It doesn't get better than this."

THE END

A NOTE FROM THE AUTHOR

Thank you so much for reading the Knight Trilogy. I really hope you've enjoyed reading it as much I have enjoyed writing it.

I'll be back in 2014 with a brand new erotic adventure to share with you all.

You can also keep up to date with my news on my facebook page, and I'm @kittysbooks on twitter.

ACKNOWLEDGMENTS

As ever, this book couldn't have happened without the help and support of some very special people.

Thanks first and foremost to Charlie Hobson, editor extraordinaire and word magician.

Also to Angela Oltmann, for being a joy to work with and for a third cover, possibly my favourite ever.

Thank you to my beautiful minxes of romance ~ the best writing buddies and friends this girl could ever wish for. I salute you.

Ditto the gorgeous ladies of Bobland ~ you know I love you all to pieces!

Special, huge thanks have to go to all of the amazing book-bloggers and Facebook groups. You guys work so hard on behalf of the authors, I'm grateful beyond words for your support and encouragement. Extra love to Gitte, Jenny and all the delicious ladies at Totally Booked, you ladies really rock my world.

Also, to all of the ladies who make every day brighter on Facebook and twitter, you are truly my cyber-sisters. Writing can be a lonely profession sometimes, but you all make it less so by being there. You make me laugh, you answer my many random research questions, you hold my hand when I'm nervous, and I've lost count of the number of glasses of wine we've shared along the way! Your support means the world to me.

Behind the scenes, I couldn't do any of this without my own special people ~ my family, my kids, and my beloved Mr.F. Special big-up to Mr.F's emerging talent in the kitchen. Who knew? I'm a lucky lady in every way. x

ABOUT THE AUTHOR

Kitty French is the USA Today best selling author of the Knight Trilogy.

She also writes romantic comedy under the pseudonym Kat French. Her debut novel, Undertaking Love, is out now from HarperCollins.

Kitty lives in England with her husband and two young sons.

Printed in Great Britain
by Amazon.co.uk, Ltd.,
Marston Gate.